THE LAST LEMURIAN

A WESTRALIAN ROMANCE

BY

G. FIRTH SCOTT

AUTHOR OF "THE TRACK OF MIDNIGHT."

LONDON

JAMES BOWDEN

10, HENRIETTA STREET, COVENT GARDEN, W.C.

1898

" ' Now, let 'em have it,' the Hatter exclaimed, as he fired
as fast as he could work his repeater."   [*Page* 32.

CONTENTS.

——

Contents.

what we thought, when one day, without a word of warning, a young, fresh-faced Englishman arrived at the head station with all the necessary documentary evidence to prove to us—that is, Tom Smiles, the manager, and myself, the overseer—that he had been sent out by Mrs. Halliday to take immediate possession from us and send us about our business.

I was having a camp, as we term it in Australia—siesta, I believe is the proper word, and with my altered position, from that of a hard-working and not too well paid overseer to a millionaire, it behoves me to be careful and guard against too free a use of the bush vernacular. But that is rather anticipating, for at present, so far as this story is concerned, I am still the hard-working, ill-paid station overseer.

I was having a camp, as I have said, one afternoon in my own quarters—a slab hut, with a canvas "stretcher" as the chief article of furniture—when Smiles disturbed me by bursting into the place.

"Halwood! Here, wake up!" he exclaimed, shaking me by the shoulder.

"All right," I answered. "What is wrong now?"

"Wrong? Why, everything's wrong," he answered excitedly.

I looked at him quietly as the thought flashed through my mind, had sober, steady-going old Smiles broken out and gone for the rum keg? —got a touch of the sun, as we should put it?

"You're sacked," he added.

It was undoubtedly a case of the sun, I thought, and to humour him I said, "All right. I suppose I can finish my camp before making tracks?"

"You're sacked," he yelled. "D'ye hear? Sacked! You, me, and the whole gang. Sacked straight off the jigger."

My reply was not perfectly polite, so I will not repeat it. Suffice it to say that it was expressive.

"Yes, young fellow; we're sacked for robbing and cheating that——" he referred to our late esteemed employeress, but he did not use her usual name.

I was too mystified to understand quite the drift of his conversation and told him so. Then he became more explicit, and after telling me about the young Englishman's arrival and the purport of his mission, he dragged me out of the hut and over to his quarters. There I found the rosy-cheeked young Englishman standing at the door, perspiring like a carcass in a boiling-down vat, and staring across the and flashing when he is aroused in temper or uses his mental powers vigorously.

I was studying him closely, so closely, indeed, that I had forgotten for the moment what I was doing, when he interrupted me with the word " Satisfied ? "

The remark nonplussed me for a moment, and before I could find words for an answer he went on with a smile :

" You're quite right, my lad ; always size up a man when you have the chance, though for my own part I prefer to do it directly I meet him. I took your measure before you got off your horse."

" Well, I was a bit struck," I began.

" Yes, I know," he interrupted. " But I was going to say something more. I took your measure, and, if I am not mistaken—and it isn't often that I am—you are just the sort that I want. I suppose you wouldn't mind a bit of rough mining, would you ? "

" I have half made up my mind to go and have a look round Coolgardie," I answered. " They say there's a good show down that way for any one who gets in ahead of the syndicators."

" Maybe there is, but I don't think much of that part myself. I've been over the country, and—well, I may be wrong, but I reckon there's going to be a lot of money dropped there, if people don't mind and watch it. That isn't my lay, though. I'm after a bigger deal, I take it, and if you care to chip in, why, I want a mate, and for my part I'm on to take on with you."

"But what's the swindle?" I asked.

"Yes, I reckoned you were going to ask that; it's in your face and I'm glad it is. I like a man to look before he leaps."

He leaned forward to knock the ashes out of his pipe.

"Just let me charge up again and I'll tell you the yarn, and then you can say whether you're on or not, and we can go into details."

I waited while he cut up his tobacco, and, filling his pipe, lit it with a glowing ember. He lay back with his arms behind his head, and his legs stretched out in front of him and commenced his story, while I listened without interrupting him.

"I said I had been over the Coolgardie country," he began. "Well, so I was about a year ago, but I found nothing more than colour here and there, though I'm free to own I did not stay long. I was making for a range that I thought looked much more likely country, when I fell in with a mob of blacks. I've picked up a bit of their jabber in different parts, and although every tribe has its own version of a language, I was able to get along fairly well with them.   My horses were a bit knocked up, and as they told me there was good feed at the place they were going to, I thought I might as well go that way too.   There was good feed at their camping ground, and I gave the horses a fortnight's spell at it, and they wanted it, I can tell you, for Westralia is rats of a place to travel in generally."

"There was a rum old chap with the tribe, and he was particularly scared of me.   I bailed him up one day and asked him what was wrong. He wouldn't speak for a time, but at last I got it out of him.   It was this way.   Once, a long time ago, when he was little more than a piccaninny, he had been away to the north-east from where we were camped, on some black fellow's trip or other.   The party he was with had struck a desert, and, if such a thing can happen to a black, had got bushed.   Anyway they wandered and wandered till they were nearly all dead, and only my old boy and two others were left, when they saw, away on the horizon, the blue shade of a range.   They made for it with all the life that was left in them, and here comes the curious part of the yarn.   When they got there they hunted around for water, which he said they had not tasted for a week, but I did not swallow that fairy tale. They found it, however, and were sleeping off the effects of their too copious libations—I have heard it said that men who are nearly dead with thirst get fairly groggy when they do reach water and drink their fill—when they were surprised by another tribe and carried off; where to, do you think ? "

" Give it up," I said.

" Well, you see how tanned I am ; I could as soon pass for a yellow as a white man, but the old boy said my colour only suggested that of the creature before whom they were taken. She was a yellow woman, as yellow as a nugget of gold, he said, and as big—oh ! I was only a baby compared to her."

He laughed as he stretched out his arms and rolled over on to his side.

" The old chap didn't have a happy time of it and took the first opportunity to clear. He didn't wait for his mates, who, he maintained, were eaten alive by this yellow female. He somehow got away, and, failing to find his way home, joined the first tribe of blacks he fell in with after his escape, and had been with them ever since. But the part of the yarn that touched me the most was that, in the range,

and friendship are all very well to talk about when there are no niggers around, but in the back blocks don't go without a revolver, and a rifle too, if you can get one."

"Then we shall want another pack horse to carry them," I said.

"And very useful he'll be when we come to load up the team with gold," he replied laughingly."

"Please yourself," I said. "It's all one to me, so long as we push along and see what there is in the yarn. If there's nothing we can always get back to Coolgardie."

"That's so," he answered. "If you don't mind, I'll do the fitting out of our party—both as regards choice and payment," he added.

"We will start fair——" I began.

"When we get to Wyunga," he interrupted. "Now we'll round up the horses and push on."

So we saddled up our horses and started ; but we were not many miles on our way when we had our first streak of luck.

We were riding along at an easy pace, the Hatter leading his pack horse, when suddenly all three animals stopped short in their stride and stood, with ears pricked up, snorting and trembling as if playing a revival of the Balaam's ass episode. I looked round for some cause of the alarm but saw nothing beyond the usual bush surroundings.

"Camels," my companion said laconically.

"What!" I exclaimed.

"Camels," he repeated, leaning forward in his saddle with his head turned on one side and apparently listening intently.

I had heard, in camp-fire yarns, about the terror which seizes on horses when first they see or smell the ship of the desert. Their introduction into Australia for service over the long waterless tracks which exist in some parts of the interior had occurred some years previously, but none had ever come my way, and my knowledge of them and their ways was purely by hearsay, but this was evidently not the case with the Hatter.

"I don't quite make it out," he said, speaking as much to the neighbouring gum trees as to me.

I was about to inquire what he meant, when he cried out: "Here, catch hold."

He moved his horses over to me and, throwing both reins into my hands, jumped from his saddle and ran quickly to a clump of gums that grew about a hundred yards from us.

From trembling the horses began to get restive, and I had a fairly warm time of it, what with my own mount, the Hatter's, and the pack horse. They kept my attention pretty well engaged, and I could only glance now and again in the direction whence the Hatter had disappeared. Presently I heard him call out to me and warn me to sit tight, and the next moment I realised the value of his advice. The deuce itself might have entered into the beasts, judging by the way they started plunging. I managed to hang on to my own ; but the pack horse jerked its reins out of my hand, and the mare the Hatter rode reared so suddenly, that the old weather-worn leather of the bridle snapped and away went both horses as fast as they could gallop. It was a good ten minutes before my own grew sufficiently tired of bucking, in a way I never knew a horse to buck before, to permit me even to look round.

Then I saw the cause of the mischief. Just beyond the clump of stunted gums stood a team of five camels, with the Hatter at the head of the leader, and holding his sides and laughing as though he were witnessing the finest pantomime ever staged.

" Stick to it, my lad ; he'll be used to them in an hour or so," he cried.

Before I had time to answer I was in the thick of another bout of bucks and pig jumps, and every other sort of eccentric motion which the mind of a horse can conceive of on the spur of the moment as a means to unseat its rider. I was a fairly good hand at riding, and could tackle an average bucker with a certain degree of safety and satisfaction ; but it would be idle to deny that I have no desire whatever for a further experience of how a bush horse greets its first introduction to the camel tribe.

It was a great contest between my capacity for sticking on and the condition of my horse, and if the latter had not given out when it did I should have voyaged into space, and, perhaps, eternity, in a couple more rounds. When it did end my horse was too fatigued even to tremble.

" Here's a throw in," the Hatter exclaimed, when I was able to get near him, and after he had expressed his entire satisfaction at my exhibition of horsemanship. " We needn't waste time over Wyunga ; we've got all the stores we want, and more too, for that matter, delivered right into our hands by the gift of Providence, or the luck of the road, as you may please to put it."

The camels, it appeared, he had found browsing peacefully with their loads on their backs, but without any signs of a driver or a

with the ants and the crows had made them gruesome objects to look at, even from the distance.

As we rode round the camp we found three more bodies, only these had been blacks and females.

" It's best to leave them as they are," the Hatter remarked coolly, as he turned his horse's head in the direction we had come from. " The old, old bush story ! They won't leave the domestic hearth of some stray nomad in peace, and then white civilisation is outraged because the blacks mete out summary jurisdiction upon the offenders."

" But it's strange they didn't plunder the team as well," I said.

" And strange they killed the women, too," he answered. " They don't often do that— unless the camels scared them. By Jove ! I never thought of that," he exclaimed, looking round at me with his face aglow. " They were scared, I've heard, of horses when they first saw them, and now they're scared of camels. But what price our chances with the yellow lady's tribe if we ride up on camels ? "

" I'd rather trust to the Winchesters if it comes to business," I said.

" Well, I'm satisfied with the camels," he answered.

CHAPTER IV.

BLACK SUFFERS.

IT seems rather lawless, looking back at it from the safety of civilisation with a policeman at the street corner, but we were at least two days' ride from the nearest habitation of a white man, and nothing whatever could have been served by riding there and telling who-ever we met of what we had found. Besides, it would have delayed us, and we were both, now that we were on the road, as impatient to get along towards that wonderful though misty range as schoolboys are to get home for the holidays. We might have buried what remained of the men who had, by chance, bequeathed us our outfit, but that would have prevented effectually any one ever finding a trace of them. So we made the best of what fate had thrown in our way. Leaving the bleaching bones to rest where they were till some one happened to come along and discover them, we formed up our enlarged cavalcade the following morning and steered for the open desert, which we knew lay right in our path.

It was the third day from our start, which we counted from the waterhole where we found the camels ; the sun was well down towards the horizon, when the Hatter, who had, it seemed to me, been very restless all the afternoon, rode up alongside of me.

"I should not be surprised if there was a row to-night," he said.

I looked round at the sky, which was without a cloud. "You don't mean thunder, do you ? " I asked.

"No, my lad ; niggers."

"Why, there isn't a sign of them, and besides, what have we to fear ? We haven't been disturbing the peace of their hearths," I answered, quoting the words he had used when we found those others poor chaps.

"There's plenty of sign, and has been all day," he said. "As to disturbing them, the previous owners of these did that," and he jerked his head towards the string of camels slouching along with their packs as stolidly and methodically as only camels can.

"It's as well to be prepared," he went on. "I reckon they're coming, and anyway there's nothing like being beforehand with niggers."

"Then we'd better take watch and watch when we camp."

"Watch and watch? No, not much. Double watch in these parts. They're mighty cunning, are the niggers you find near Spinifex Deserts, and that is the country we are coming to. I've got a little plan for them which I reckon will just about collapse them."

It was a pretty little plan too, when he described it. We were to camp at just such a place as afforded them (if his surmise were correct and blackfellows were about) splendid cover from which to make their attack. They would creep up and spear us as we lay around the fire or sat yarning, he explained, but in order to run them into their own snare, we would, carefully watching that we were not observed, fix up two dummy figures under the blankets and leave them by the fire, while we, with our Winchesters and plenty of spare cartridges (both of which we drew from our camel-packs) would be resting elsewhere with an open range on to the cover we left convenient for the attackers.

We shortly afterwards came upon just such a spot as we wanted. The country, which had been rather broken earlier in the day, opened out into a small level patch, free from timber except about the middle, where some scattered bushes grew in front of a few gums. On the left of the bushes and a little behind them a shallow ridge shot out like a tongue from the rougher and more thickly timbered country we had been travelling over.

" This is our place !" the Hatter exclaimed. " They'll follow close on our tracks, so we'll steer straight across to the other side of the bushes. We'll light our fire there, right ahead from here, so that it will show the shelter of the bushes, and, if I am not mistaken, draw them clean up to the trap. They'll be bound to creep up under the cover and have a shy at us—only we shall be on that rise on your left, where we can see them a bit clearer than they can see us."

It did not take us long to reach our ground and get our camp fixed up, and by the time the sun was sinking we had it all ready, even to our lay figures. We kept on the move enough to stop them making any attempt to cross the open ground between the broken country and the bushes, but as soon as the dark came we crept along the ground away from where our fire was blazing towards the tongue of the ridge. We had stacked our packs up so as to make a streak of shadow in the gleam of the fire, and this and the occasional impedimenta of tree stems and bushes effectually screened our movements from observation. When we reached the rising ground we crept back as far as we could with safety to our shelter, and lay, with our rifles ready, barely fifty yards from the bushes, on the other side of which the fire was blazing.

We had thrown some heavy logs on the fire before we left, so that the flames should not be too bright while we crossed to our place of vantage. They were now beginning to get well alight, and although we were in deep shadow we could see distinctly everything on the open patch between the bushes and the timber. We lay very still, and as the minutes went by and no sound came to us save the crackle of the fire and an occasional noise as the camels and horses moved, I began to grow sceptical of the Hatter's opinion. I was not used to watching under arms, and the experience prompted all sorts of foolish actions. First, I was tempted to tell my companion all I thought about his suspicions, and only the memory of his earnest request for absolute silence restrained me. Then there came a great desire to jump up, and run, and again to let off my rifle " just for a lark," as a schoolboy would say. I fought all and each and several more equally senseless ideas in turn and the hours went on, but no blackfellows showed where we anticipated they would. I was beginning to grow drowsy, and rested my head on my arms for a moment. It could not have been more, I am convinced, although the Hatter maintained afterwards that I had been asleep for over an hour, when I felt a gentle push on my shoulder. I raised my head, but before I could quite grasp the scene I heard a low whisper.

"Steady! Take from the right Fire when I say."

Straight in front of me, standing in a half-circle behind the bushes, was a row of black fellows, their bodies all streaked and spotted with ochre, upon which the firelight, now con-siderably diminished, glowed in an uncanny way. Each man held a long war spear in his right hand, the ugly barbed points indicating like finger posts where our two lay figures rested under the blankets. Every warrior stood as still as the trees, not a muscle quivering nor a limb moving, but with the whole frame in a position which denoted more powerfully than the wildest movement a readiness to strike that was, even in the situation we were in, grandly impressive. I almost forgot that I was popularly supposed to be one of the figures half the spears were levelled at till I heard that soft whisper again.

" Have you covered him ? "

It was my first taste of man-shooting and, had there been time, I should have cared for it less than I did. An uneasy tremor passed over me, and I remember I set my teeth very hard as I brought the sights of my rifle in line with the magnificent frame of the warrior on the extreme right. But, after all, I was only doing to him as he would do to me, and that idea gave me resolution for the moment.

" When they throw."

The whisper scarcely reached me ere, by some preconceived signal which was invisible to us, each spear was hurled through the bushes and buried itself in mine or the Hatter's blankets. I needed no further stimulus, and it was with a feeling of savage delight that I pressed the trigger home, my delight becoming elation as I saw my target leap in the air and fall lifeless.

Our shots must have been a terrible mystery to those unfortunates, for they stood as if they were too much amazed to move for the moment. Then they saw two of their number, the men who had stood at either end of their line, lying lifeless on the ground, and with one accord they crowded round them in two groups.

and almost before I could realise it a stretch of fair green verdure seemed to rise from amidst the sand, and I was shot from my seat as my camel sank on its knees beside a clear pool of water. My head was in it, and I was swallowing great gulps of it, too, a second later.

Some one seized me by the legs and pulled me away from it, and I turned with hot words on my lips to see the Hatter standing over me and smiling.

" Wait till I brew some tea, my lad, or you'll get as drunk as the blackfellows I told you about," he said.

I sat up and looked at him blankly. My memory came back in a rush. It was only just now that I had been reviling him for leading me into a waterless, arid desert to die and leave my bones to whiten, and yet here I was resting in the shade of broad-leaved trees with sweet grass growing under me, and a wide pool of clear water, some of which still clung to my hair and beard, beside me.

" Am I mad or dreaming ? " I exclaimed.

" Neither, my lad ; only you were getting a bit down a day or so ago, so to save trouble to both of us I sent you off."

" Sent me off ? " I repeated.

" Yes. It's all right. I had to do it," he

said laughing. " I'm a bit of a hypnotist, you know," he added.

It was a new word to me then, but it struck me as being a strange sort of proceeding, and I said so.

" Well, we'll discuss that later," he answered. " For the present let us camp."

Whatever he was he had me under his thumb, for I had to do just as he pleased, whether I wanted to or not.

After we had finished our meal—a meal by the way that was the sweetest I had ever enjoyed —we lit our pipes, and he explained something of what he meant. I gathered that he had a control over me, and that, if he liked, he could make me do anything he wished ; but, he said, he was not going to use it so long as I stood by him, as I had said I would.

" We've come so far together, not without danger and difficulty," he said. " But if my anticipations are right, and this is the range the old blackfellow told me of, we may have many more to face before we start back with our camels loaded up with gold. Are we still mates ? "

There was no getting away from the frankness of his eyes, and, half-ashamed of myself, I held out my hand.

" Mates to the end," I answered.

when it meets the sand, just as if it were trimmed every morning. Why, there are no birds about the place, nor flies, nor anything else that I can see with life, except the trees and the grass."

It was quite correct. We hunted through the trees for a sign of some token of animal life, but beyond our camels and ourselves there was none. In our search we came up to the rock down which the water tumbled. We understood then why it had worn away so little, for not even with the aid of a chilled steel drill and a heavy hammer could we make more than the faintest impression upon it.

"If this is our golden range and we have to mine in stuff like this, I'm afraid it will be a long time before we get our camels loaded," I said, as we rested from our fruitless efforts. "We could have driven a hole a foot deep in the toughest rock I ever met with by this time, and there is hardly a dent in this, and the point flattened off the drill into the bargain."

"It *is* a quaint place, and I should not be surprised even if we met the Yellow Lady of twenty feet stature, and her hordes of shrivelled-up mummies," the Hatter answered, looking at the rock with a puzzled expression on his face.

"I wonder what dynamite would do," I suggested.

"Not worth wasting it. We may need all we have before we get to the end of our journey," he answered.

"I don't feel altogether comfortable," I said, as I rose from the boulder I had been sitting upon. There was a strange oppressiveness in the air now that the first effects of the charm were wearing away. "I'm inclined to over-haul our rifles and sort out the ammunition. We may want them before long."

The Hatter looked at me with a smile lurking away down in the depths of his eyes.

"Getting nervous?" he asked.

"Not exactly, but——what's that?"

If ever I felt my heart in my mouth it was at that moment. The Hatter jumped to his feet with the blaze in his eyes that always came when he was suddenly startled, and I felt braver when I saw that he too had felt the shock.

We had been resting with our backs to the pool, and a heavy plunge and its accompanying splash, that sounded terribly loud in the quiet of the place, had been the cause of our alarm. We hurried to the pool.

A few bubbles still floating on the surface

and the race of ripples travelling from the centre to the sides were all we could discern.

The Hatter stood watching the pool, calm and unconcerned again, while I looked anywhere and everywhere for some explanation of the mystery.

"It is too absurd," I heard the Hatter say, and then he laughed, and I turned towards him.

"But we'll get our rifles all the same," he went on, looking round at me.

"Why, what do you make of it?" I asked, as we hastened to the spot where we had piled the packs when we lifted them off the backs of our tired camels.

"Bunyip," he answered. "Look at the camels."

The creatures that we had left browsing peacefully in the shade of the trees when we went to test the quality of the rock were now standing out in the sunlight on the desert, their necks swaying from side to side and their big blabby lips shaking, while their eyes rolled and glared in every direction.

"Here, let's get out of this," I cried, a horrible tremor of fear running over me.

The Hatter did not answer, but walked to the packs and drew out the rifles. Then he opened the box of ammunition and handed me a packet of cartridges.

"Load up the magazine, and put the rest in your pocket," he said, as he proceeded to set me the example.

When we had finished filling the Winchesters, the Hatter produced two revolvers, which were also in the armoury of our treasure-trove camel train. We took one each, carefully loading all the chambers and keeping some spare cartridges in our pockets.

"Now we can look to the camels," the Hatter said.

We went to them and tried to soothe the terror they evidently felt. They came to meet us, and followed us as far as the beginning of the grass, but nothing we could do would induce them to come off the sand.

"It's no use wasting time over them. Let's go back and wait," the Hatter said.

"But what have we got to wait for?" I asked.

"The bunyip," he answered laconically.

"Oh! go slow!" I exclaimed. "You don't believe that silly yarn, do you?"

"My lad, I'm ready to believe anything about this place after the rock and that splash. The old man swore the pool he and his fellow niggers drank out of was the bunyip's lair, and that was why they all went to sleep. If this isn't the place and the range he talked about, then it's another equally peculiar. I've always thought there must be something in the bunyip yarn."

I laughed. "You're as bad as a new chum," I exclaimed.

"Wait awhile," he replied. "You've heard the yarn the same as I have, and I suppose every other white man has who ever saw or spoke to an aboriginal. Only, perhaps, I have heard it more often, because I have had more to do with blackfellows, and that in every part of the continent, from York Peninsula to Wilson's Promontory, and from the Swan river to Moreton Bay."

"That's a pretty stiff bit of country," I interrupted.

"It includes what I say—every part of the continent," he continued quietly. "Now just add this up, and see what it comes to. From every blackfellow who has told me the yarn—and there have been a few hundreds of them—the description has always been the same. You can't talk about collusion between men and tribes who never saw or heard of one another. Firstly, they're all scared out of their lives of it. 'Baal th'at pfeller bunyip; 'im no good, 'im debbil-debbil,' they tell you, if they talk what they call English. If they don't, they tell you the same in their own tongue. They've never seen it, but—and this is the second point—they tell you it lives in deep waterholes and lagoons, and for that reason they will never go into strange water nor camp near it, and sometimes will go for days without a drink rather than visit a pool where the bunyip is said to be."

"No one has ever seen one since the white man came here, at all events," I answered.

"Well?"

"And they've looked often enough. Why, scares are always getting up about the bunyip being heard or seen in some lagoon or other, and all the country side turns out and hunts, and hunts, and hunts, but nary a bunyip can be found."

"Well?" he repeated.

"Well, isn't that enough? If it isn't, how do you get over the fact that these scares get up at places hundreds, and sometimes thousands, of miles apart? Does the bunyip fly, or are there more than one, and if there are, why hasn't——"

"There is only one," he interrupted.

" Then how does he travel from one place to another ? " I said.

" Look here, my lad, the water from that pool goes somewhere, doesn't it ? "

" I suppose so," I replied.

" And so does the water of hundreds of other pools and rivers in Australia—but it does not flow on the surface. Why should there not be underground channels leading from one to the other, and perhaps ending or centring here, for example, as an ideal bunyip's lair ? "

" That's too stiff for me ! " I exclaimed.

" All right ; we'll wait and see," he answered.

We dropped the discussion, and turned to consider our plan of campaign. I could not accept the bunyip theory, but at the same time there was no questioning the fact that something very mysterious had occurred when we heard that splash, or why should the camels be so terrified?

" I fancy the trees," I exclaimed, looking up into the leafy canopy of one. " If we get up above the lower branches the leaves will screen us from below, while we can see all that goes on, and have a grand command over any enemy underneath us."

" It's a stiff climb," the Hatter answered,

looking at the trunk, which rose a good thirty feet without a twig to mar its smoothness.

"I think I can do it," I answered, for I was always a great hand at climbing, and rather plumed myself upon my prowess.

"But I doubt if I can," the Hatter said.

"Why, there's that rope ladder in the tool kit that we were nearly throwing away," I exclaimed, suddenly remembering the article which had caused us some wonder as to the reason of its inclusion in a miner's swag when we first found it.

"Our luck again," he answered, as we over-hauled the packs until we came to the one we wanted. Taking a coil of light lanyard with me, and leaving my rifle at the foot of the tree (I did not care to go up without my revolver, in case I should meet anything unexpected), I started to swarm up the tree. It was, as the Hatter had remarked, a stiff climb, but I did it, although when I reached the lower branches I was pretty well blown. I threw one leg over a bough, and, holding on to the trunk of the tree, I examined the situation.

The leaves grew thick almost to the stem, and about six feet above me another set of branches shot out from the trunk. The bough upon which I rested forked out into two prongs, as it were, some three feet from the trunk of the tree, and each of these again forked a foot farther on. Growing laterally, the twigs and minor branches formed a perfect network of stems, with the leaves so thick that it was difficult to see through, and impossible for any one to fall through them to the ground. The branches which stood out all round were equally dense, and I called out to the Hatter that I had found a place where we could almost stow the camels.

Climbing on to the boughs I lowered my line, which he made fast to one end of the ladder, and I soon had it up. The other end lay on the ground in a coil, so I clambered up to the second tier of branches and made my end fast there. Then I called out to the Hatter to come up.

He came up and inspected.

" We'll fix our camp up here," he said, " and I reckon all the bunyips in the world won't reach us."

The sun was getting down towards the horizon, so that we had not much time. We made the most of it, however, and when it went down, we had all our ammunition and blankets up in our nest, besides food and water, to last us for a day or so. While we still had light we bent some of the boughs so as to enable us to have a clear view of the ground and the pool below us.

The moon was at the full, and as the sun went out of sight it rose. Out on the desert we could see our camels grouped together and crouched down as if asleep. The pool, lit up into a silver sheen, rested unruffled below us, and between the dense foliage of the trees the moonlight streamed upon an open patch of closely growing grass immediately in front of our look-out holes. Everywhere else the shadow was impenetrable.

We had taken a hasty meal, and now lay prone upon our blankets, with rifles ready, waiting and watching for anything which might eventuate.

The subdued tinkle of the falling water was the only sound to be heard, and the weird stillness of the scene was beginning to affect me more than I appreciated, when suddenly we heard a heavy grating noise from somewhere in the darkness beyond the trees.

The Hatter touched me, and I turned my face towards him.

"There's something in the air I can't make out," he whispered.

"Where?" I asked in the same tone, and looking quickly round.

reached to her knees, but as we watched them more closely we saw that they were men, small, wizened, shrivelled-up men, and involuntarily the expression of the Hatter's blackfellow came to my mind. They were moving and living copies of sun-dried mummies!

She waved her arms, and the swarm scattered round the pool until they stood, a ring of withered gnomes, at the edge of the water.

She clapped her hands, and the figures, stooping down as if impelled by one instinct, began to beat the surface of the water with both hands, so fast that it was soon a white foaming cauldron.

Again she clapped her hands, and the beating ceased, every little figure standing still and silent, so still that we could hear the bubbles bursting in a soft hissing sound.

The woman stood gazing intently upon the pool until the last of the foam had vanished. Then again she clapped her hands, and again the throng of figures beat the water till it frothed, and again she waited till the foam had disappeared. Three times was the performance repeated before she uttered a sound. Then as the last bubble burst she spoke.

I do not know what she said, but with the first word the Hatter exclaimed, " Ah."

I suppose it was due to the strain upon my nerves, and the intentness with which I had been watching the scene, but the sound of the Hatter's voice startled me so suddenly that I clutched my hands in sheer fright. I was holding my rifle with a finger on the trigger, and the result was a shot.

It rang out upon the night, the flash of the powder gleamed in the dark, and the bullet plunged into the middle of the pool. I heard the Hatter make a startled exclamation, and the rest was a wild nightmare.

The woman, turning her frightful eyes towards our hiding-place, raised her arms to their full length over her head with her fingers extended, and uttered a long, low wail, that horrified me and terrified me nearly to a stupor. The swarm of pigmies scattered from the pool, and ran hither and thither through the trees, making inarticulate sounds that were as though an army were gurgling in the last agonies of convulsions.

I felt the Hatter's hand grip my wrist, and in my ear I heard him whisper—

" Fool, sleep."

Then darkness fell upon me.

It seemed an age by the time that I recovered my senses, although the Hatter told me it was only a few minutes.

I heard his voice in my ear—

" Lie still, and fear nothing "

" All right," I whispered back, and at once I felt cool and collected.

Below me the woman still stood wailing, and round and round the pool the pigmy figures were pattering.

" Listen," the Hatter whispered again. " I think I know her language, and I'm going to play a bold stroke."

" All right," I answered. They were the only words I seemed to know.

For the account of the following scene, so far as the dialogue is concerned, I am entirely indebted to my companion, the language in which it was conducted being to me merely an aimless babble of sounds, without accent, rhythm, or anything else that distinguishes the chatter of apes from human speech. The Hatter told me afterwards that it was the tongue of a tribe he had come across somewhere in the Pitchorie district, a tract of country in North Australia, hundreds of miles from anywhere save desert, where the blacks find their much-valued narcotic, the pitchorie plant.

Leaning over his loophole the Hatter called out in a loud voice :

She stood up again, her eyes flaring in a fresh horror.

" I name him. Bunyip ! "

The pigmies seemed to shrink into yet smaller and more repulsive forms at the mention of the word, and she who uttered it crouched down upon the ground till her wealth of hair spread over her and hid the glaring yellow skin from our eyes, while sobs shook her frame and added still more to the weird, unearthly spectacle below us.

" Go back from whence you came. Rest hidden till the moon comes up again. Then come here once more."

She pushed back the hair from her face as she looked up.

" My destiny, O king," she said.

" Learn it then."

With a cry she sprang to her feet, and the pigmies, galvanised, as it were, into life by her voice, jumped up and rushed away into the shadows from whence they first appeared. She waited till they had gone, and then, turning towards our hiding place, she bowed seven times to the ground before she followed her army into the darkness.

Again we heard the grating sound, and then the night was silent.

" My lad, we don't know what they are, let alone what they have been," he said seriously. " The aboriginals in their present state are mysterious enough, but the race we are now dealing with surpasses anything that I ever heard of."

" Well, supposing there is a secret door or entrance through the rock, how are we going to find it out, and what are we going to do when we have found it ? " I asked. The Hatter had a solemn way of talking when he started on the aboriginal topic, and could bring out so many strange and forcible arguments on his side of the question that I knew it was no use my continuing the discussion. What I wanted to see was the gold, and what I wanted to do was to get back to civilisation with it as soon as possible. I had had more than enough of uncanny experiences.

The Hatter smoked for some minutes before he answered my queries.

"That is just the problem I'm trying to solve," he said at length. " I'll tell you my idea and then we can discuss it in detail."

He unfolded his plan, and as I listened I was amazed at the extraordinary fertility of his mental resources. What would have taken me years to evolve he reeled off as fast as he could speak, and sometimes faster than I could understand.

"What a genius you are!" I exclaimed when he had finished.

"Nonsense!" he answered. "What has already occurred is the basis of my idea, and I merely elaborate the possibilities arising therefrom. Do you agree with my scheme?"

"Indeed I do," I answered, and, as it worked out without a hitch, I will not anticipate, but content myself with describing it in the order of its unfolding.

With the dawn we descended from our nest and cautiously approached the horrible creature we had killed during the night. Our caution was unnecessary, for it was stone dead, with bullet-holes all over it. Closer inspection showed it to be even more repulsive than it had appeared to be when first it rose to the surface of the pool, and it was a relief when, in accordance with the Hatter's scheme, we covered it over with a blanket and hid its gruesome proportions from our sight. Upon the blanket we scattered grass and leaves until that too was hidden.

We next turned our attention to our camels, They were still huddled into a group away out on the desert, where we had seen them the previous night, and, failing in our endeavours to lead them back to the grass, we had to cut and carry some of it out to where they were. Having attended to their wants, we satisfied our own, and then proceeded to follow along the track our visitors had made through the scrub. As the Hatter had foreseen, it ended at what to all appearances was a solid wall of rock.

"Now for our preparations," the Hatter exclaimed, when we had satisfied ourselves that we could never hope to find out by ourselves how that rock moved. We returned to the pool and worked steadily till the sun was well overhead, and with everything arranged to our satisfaction for the evening's performance of what the Hatter termed our one-act comedy, we climbed up to our nest and took advantage of the opportunity to make up for the loss of the previous night's sleep.

The sun was sinking in the west when the Hatter awakened me, and together we sat and waited for the moon to rise and the Yellow Woman to come. To me the time seemed to drag, until minutes grew to hours, and my nerves were strained to their utmost long before we heard the grating noise which indicated the approach of the unearthly-looking creature we awaited. The Hatter leaned over to me and whispered :—

" You must be perfectly cool and collected."

" I'll try," I answered uneasily.

" You must," he hissed in my ear, and I felt my heart grow steady. It was well that he had strength of will enough for both.

" Aim over her heart, but keep your finger off the trigger until I cry out; then fire," he said, just as the gleam of phosphorescent light glimmered through the trees.

A moment later the weird, majestic form appeared, and walked almost on to the blanket that covered the other horror.

" Stand and wait," the Hatter cried out in the—to me—meaningless jargon.

Immediately she stopped, and I, resting my rifle along the boughs, took a careful and steady aim.

" Who am I ? " the Hatter asked.

" The King of Night," she answered, turning her ghastly eyes up towards our hiding place.

" Why come you ? "

" O mighty one, was I not promised that to-night I should learn my destiny ? I have come, as you commanded, to learn. O mighty one, speak on."

Her eyes were almost pathetic as she spoke

5

and, extending her arms towards us, she sank down upon her knees.

"First, must you see him whom you named to me," the Hatter cried, and, pulling a line we had fastened to the blanket, he scattered the leaves and the grass, and exposed the dead horror to the woman's gaze.

The agony of the cry with which she greeted it made my heart bleed for her. Her unearthly surroundings and appearance were for the moment forgotten in the perfectly human anguish she displayed.

She had fallen forward upon the body, and was moaning piteously.

"Seek you to know your destiny," he cried.

She raised her face towards us, and the misery written upon it was too real for us to doubt the profundity of her grief.

"Oh! what is my destiny to the loss of the companion of centuries and the solace of my solitude?" she answered, and buried her face in her hands.

"Listen and know. Weep while you may, for in a vision shall even now appear before you the image of your lord. Strive not to touch him or you die. Before you he shall rise. His eyes shall see you and his ears shall hear you, but his mouth shall be closed. From afar he comes to seek you. Tell him then your history. Unfold to him the secret of the rock, and, as a token and a guide, when the vision is before you, go to your myrmidons and bid them build above the dead one a pile of the shining yellow stones that lie within the wall."

She listened as he spoke, her eyes gleaming and flickering, and when he ceased she looked around.

"O mighty one, where comes the vision? I see it not."

"Weep while you may," the Hatter answered; and she, looking down upon the lifeless creature again, renewed her lamentations, spreading her hair about her and hiding her face from sight.

Silently the Hatter lowered the ladder, and climbing down, crept along to the opposite side of the pool. With my heart thumping against my ribs I waited until he stood full in the moonlight, his magnificent form drawn up to its full height, his face raised towards the light, and his arms folded across his chest. Then, with my right hand on my rifle, ready to fire if necessary, and my gaze fixed upon the woman, I reached out with my other hand to where my revolver was strapped to the branch and pulled the trigger.

With a scream of mingled fear and rage the woman sprang to her feet, her eyes glaring up towards me. Then, as if controlled by some subtle power, she looked across the pool to where the Hatter stood. For a moment she stood as if carved in stone.

Throwing wide open her arms, she took one step forward, her face transformed by the look of ineffable love that swept over it.

"My love, my life! Ah! come to me," she cried, and I, fearing she might forget the Hatter's warning and rush towards him, brought my rifle to bear upon her heaving breast, at the same time giving vent to the best imitation I could produce of what I thought a god-like growl of disapprobation ought to be.

Without removing her gaze from the Hatter, she said (so he told me afterwards),

"O mighty one, fear not. I will not seek to touch the vision."

But she looked at it—looked until I thought she was never going to speak or move again—and all the time the Hatter stood like a statue.

"Loved one, who seek for me, knowing not my resting place, keep wide your ears that I may teach you where to find me, how to know me—even though you come from whence the anger came that doomed our race to woe."

With many movements and a wealth of dramatic action, but always with her gaze fixed upon him, she told, without a pause, the following extraordinary story to the Hatter :—

"Loved one, I am Tor Ymmothe, the Queen of Lemuria.

"Once, where those deserts lie, waved fair gardens. Mighty palaces rose from amidst the scented forests, and we, a mighty people, knew of nothing mightier. Only the sun scorned our bidding and the moon ignored our mandates, and the king, my father, hurled at them his wrath.

"From afar there came a stranger, a man whose skin was not as ours, but yet who spoke with our tongue. He came before the king, my father, and rebuked him. He, the unknown stranger, rebuked the king, my father, who was the king of kings.

"Thus he spake : 'King, only a man thou art ; different from the beasts ; distinct from the trees ; unlike the creatures of the pool. Yet only a man, sharing with them the government of time and the monarchy of death.'

"And the king, my father, laughed, and those around him laughed, as he said, 'If I am but a man, I will create that which shall be more than man, for he shall rule both on the earth

the gigantic figure of the woman towered above a seething sea of black, moving life. Each one as he came from the shadow carried what looked to me like yellow bricks, which he threw down upon the prostrate form of the bunyip until, as we watched, the pile grew higher and higher, and the last of the hideous creature was hidden. Still the swarming thousands worked, and the yellow heap came to a point. Then they laid their burdens on the ground, retiring, as the yellow pathway grew, farther into the shade. At length there were none in view, and the Yellow Woman stood alone.

"Tell him, O mighty one, that it is done, and I await his coming," she said, looking up again.

"He comes on the wings of the wind. Await him within the secret gate, nor let it open till he calls," the Hatter answered.

She smiled towards us, and stretching out her arms, bowed to the ground seven times before she turned and walked along the shining yellow path into the shadows.

CHAPTER VII.

THE CRY OF THE SOUTHERN LAND.

It was gold—all solid, rich blocks of bright, gleaming gold—and we were rich beyond the madness of avarice, for in that heap and along that pathway there were tons and tons of it.

In a fever of excitement I urged the Hatter to load up the camels and start away at once, and then come back again with hundreds of camels and take all our gold away.

"Our gold," I shouted; "our tons and tons of gold."

He was disgustingly unaffected.

"One camel load is more than you will ever spend," he answered. "Let us leave something of her token to ease her sorrow through the——"

He broke off and turned aside. I looked at him amazed. Had it been other than the calm-minded Hatter, I should have said he broke off with a sob.

"We had better camp till the dawn," he went on.

"Why, there's the sun coming up now," I cried, pointing to the glowing east.

He had been the unquestioned leader of our little party up to that morning, but the events of the previous night had had a terrible effect upon him, and I had to assume command over him before he was inclined to do anything. I only had one idea, and that was to load up all we could of the gold on our five camels and start at once for settled country. My enthusiasm revived him to a certain extent, for I was going to sacrifice everything for the gold, and even leave food and water behind so as to give each of the camels a full load of the yellow bricks instead.

The Hatter objected to that. A camel for each of us, we carrying food and water beside us, was the arrangement he proposed, the other three to be loaded with gold, and, to hasten our departure, I agreed. When the sun was sinking in the west that night only a faint blue line on the horizon told us where the ruined wall of the Lemurian Palace guarded its incalculable wealth of bullion.

Steadily we journeyed on, the Hatter recovering his former manner as we gradually approached near to civilisation and left the mystery of the Yellow Woman farther and farther behind. Soon we ceased almost to speak of her, or the dead bunyip resting beneath his imperial tomb of wealth.

We had a more fascinating subject—the future. We tried to calculate our riches. I hazarded half a million between us, but the Hatter laughed at the idea.

"You'll be a millionaire all right, my lad," he said. But I did not understand his meaning then.

We reached timbered country in course of time, without any adventures worth mentioning, and a few days later picked up the track of a dray. Now a new difficulty presented itself to us. How were we going to get our gold disposed of in safety?

To let it be known that we were driving a gold-laden team would be to bring upon our heels every man in the district, and, besides running the risk of having our riches stolen from us, would subject us to an amount of questioning that would make our lives a burden to us. We debated the point long and earnestly, and at last decided that in the morning the Hatter should follow along the dray track till he came up with some one who could tell him where we were, and which way we were to travel to reach the nearest township with a bank in it. In the meantime I was to camp with the team.

He was away two days, and when he got back it was with the news that we were within a few days' ride of Coolgardie.

"That will suit us just as well as anywhere else," he said. "We can arrange to get the stuff into the bank without letting any one know till it's in, and then we can spin them yarns about the ranges in the south-east."

So we arranged it, and once more we had luck with us; for the day we rode into the flat, straggling, fever-stricken camp of Coolgardie most of the miners were away at a reported wonderful discovery to the north, where men could make their five ounces a day at dry blowing. We had all our stuff weighed and banked before they came back, cursing the man who first spread the rumour. We left that night for Perth, and by the time that our deposit became public news we were far enough away to escape from the badgering and questioning we should have had to face had we remained in the township. As it was, our deposit went to swell the total amount of gold won on the field, and, I dare say, played no inconsiderable part in the flotation of many a Coolgardie property upon distant markets, and amongst sublimely trusting investors.

We hastened on to Perth, and from there to Albany, where we joined a mail steamer bound for Adelaide. The previous occasion of my being in that interesting city of churches was when I was poor and unknown. Now I was the proud possessor of a deposit receipt for over a million sterling and in banking circles, at all events, a person of much interest.

We made ourselves as comfortable as our wealth enabled us to, the Hatter insisting, however, upon avoiding all suggestion of ostentation. I fear I should have done what the Americans term " spread myself " if he had not been with me, but as all the money was banked in my name (he still remaining the Hatter) and I had to act as treasurer in meeting all our bills, it went against my conscience to force any expenditure upon him, or rather his money.

The next question that we considered was where we should go to spend our princely incomes to the best advantage, for I never looked upon what we had brought away with us as our capital. The golden pile beside that silent pool across the desert was too prominently before my eyes for that.

We discussed the matter frequently and lengthily before anything was decided upon, the Hatter insisting that to purchase a good station and settle down as squatters was the best course to adopt, while I was equally persistent in urging a visit to Europe, and, to use a colonialism, having a " fair old tear round." It was no easy task to persuade my comrade to come to my way of thinking, and I had almost despaired of ever doing so when, one day, he announced his acceptance of my scheme.

A two-berth cabin was at once secured in one of the mail steamers which would shortly be passing the Semaphore on her way to London, and for the sake of convenience, we journeyed down from Adelaide on the day she was to arrive, proposing to have our last dinner on Australian soil at the hotel which overlooks the roadstead.

The Hatter had interested me more than ever of late. His reputation as a wealthy man, combined with his magnificent physique and handsome appearance, made him a notable and popular figure amongst the Adelaide people, especially with those of the feminine persuasion. He was continually in request, and had he been so minded, the fairest of South Australia's daughters would have mated with him for the asking. But he never asked. In the midst of his admirers, he was always diffident and reserved, and his very coldness added zest to the paying of homage to him, until I sometimes feared that he, being a man, could no longer resist, and that I should, after all, voyage to England alone.

We had finished our dinner and sat smoking and thinking in silence, our minds too full, I suppose, for conversation. From our window we could see on one side the wide, smooth bay, with ships lying at anchor, and beyond them the faint blue shade of Kangaroo Island away on the horizon ; on the other side, the ranges around and behind Adelaide stood out in purple distinctness, and towards the west the sky was growing lurid with the colour of the setting sun.

" This is our last meal together here," he said suddenly.

" Till we come back," I laughed, in answer.

He looked at me steadily for a minute or so with those great solemn eyes of his.

" You've been a good mate, Dick, my lad, and I thank you for it."

I glanced at his face, wondering what he was going to say next.

" I mean you never tried to get beyond

the mystery of the Hatter," he said, with a smile.

"I took you at your word, and I don't regret it either," I answered.

"And now I'm going to redeem it," he went on. "Never mind dates and names, but before I came to this country I was known by a name which you will find emblazoned in English history for centuries back. I held a title which was amongst the proudest, if not amongst the highest, in the land—and I dragged it to the gutter."

He stopped with a heavy frown on his brows, and I held my peace, waiting for him to go on.

"I came here with one idea, to amass wealth and go back and regild the shrine I had stripped."

"And you can do it," I exclaimed.

"Yes, I can do it; but I do not want to now."

"Don't want to?" I echoed.

"No, my lad, don't want to, and don't mean to."

"But our cabin——"

"You use it alone."

"Then there's the money. It is all in my name."

"And will remain so. You will use that, too."

"Oh, but I——," I began impatiently.

"My lad, you do not understand," he interrupted. "My mind is made up. All that we have brought down here is yours entirely and absolutely. To-night we part; you to voyage to other countries, I to remain in Australia. Don't try to persuade me to change my mind. It is impossible."

"But why?" I asked.

He smiled as he answered me.

"In memory of our companionship I will tell you. In this country there is a woman——"

"Ah!" I exclaimed.

"Whom I love," he continued. "Where she is I must be. I cannot leave her. Where she waits, there must I go, surrendering all else, forgetting all else, to dree my weird and hers."

A light broke in upon me. Leaping from my chair I cried, "Not——"

"Tor Ymmothe, Queen of Lemuria," he answered quietly.

I stood speechless. Such an idea had never crossed my mind. A hundred fancies throbbed through my brain and whirled my senses into confusion. Dimly I felt him take my hand,

6

and saw his eyes, lit with a strange and wonderful glow, looking into mine.

"To liberate her from the thraldom I have imposed ; to lift the curse of ages from her soul ; to bring back the breath of life once more to those who, with her, are doomed, I go —for life, for love, for destiny."

He stood between me and the window, and the rich red light of the blazing west streamed round him as I looked.

"Do not seek to change me ; do not waste words or reasons," he went on, speaking slowly and softly. "The desire has been with me since I gave her that promise. I have fought with it, and tried to conquer it, but in vain. A man may not cheat his destiny."

"You cannot go back now," I exclaimed. "We are mates to the end."

"And the end is not yet," he interrupted. "To-night we part; perhaps for ever, perhaps for a time only. You will go to Europe and enjoy the fortune you have made; I will go— where destiny decrees."

"But it is folly; blind, senseless folly. You can never reach that place alone. Come with me now; and in a year, if you wish it, we will come back together. You must think of your——"

' I have thought," he answered quickly.

"No; you have only been dreaming. It is only some fancy that has taken possession of you. A change of scene will destroy it. The sight of your old home, of your old friends, will show you the folly of it."

"Where is my old home? Where are my old friends?" he said, with a ring of sadness in his voice. "Who can say that all are not in the bygone remnant of Lemuria?"

"Nonsense," I exclaimed curtly.

"And maybe your own as well," he continued

I laughed as he spoke.

"I certainly do not remember them," I said.

"No; men do not remember through the mists of ages while the scales of blindness are on their eyes; but sometimes the scales fall, and then they see and understand."

A remark more tinged with levity than metaphysics rose to my lips, but before I could utter it he took my hand in his.

"Good-bye," he said softly. "Somewhere and sometime we shall meet again, as we have met before, at destiny's decree. Till then, farewell."

An eerie sense stole over me, and drove back the inclination to laugh and jest at him. It was as though I had suddenly become enveloped in a mist, through which I vainly strove to look. Then I turned to answer him—but he was gone.

I hastened from the room to seek him, but my efforts were useless. I sought him in the hotel and out of it, without the slightest success. The steamer was leaving in the morning, and when I failed to find him I posted to Adelaide, in the hopes of finding him there. Throughout the night I searched, but always in vain; and at last I abandoned the chase and went on board the steamer.

Now, a year later, in the metropolis of the world, surrounded by every luxury that wealth can command, I am restless and impatient. From over the miles of water that lie between me and the far-off Southern Land, the voices of the lonely bush are calling; the scent of the eucalypt comes in memory to my nostrils, and I pant and long for just one breath of the hot, dry air of the free and glorious land. Visions of " golden-haired September," when the wattles gleam and spangle through the scanty-foliaged gums, and the dill-birds call and answer from the shadows of the scrub, pass through my yearning brain, and I long for the lonely freedom of the old rough life again. Just one glimpse of a dusty track, with the blazing sun overhead ; a throat growing dry, and a skin tanned and moist ; a reckless, careless future ahead, and a jumbled past behind——it's a vagabond life, but it *is* a life, and I would give all London's joys for just such a glimpse and a billy of tea shared with a mate on the road.

It comes back to me now, clearer and more assertive than ever. To check it I wrote this yarn——and now it is stronger than before. Is it the weird attraction of that strangely sombre land or the will of the Hatter that is drawing me ? In the midst of revelry and feasting it comes to me ; when I am alone it controls me ——this fierce, wild longing to go back.

Surely I, too, do not love the Queen of Lemuria ?

CHAPTER VIII.

THROUGH THE MISTS OF TIME.

ANOTHER year has passed since I vainly strove to ease the longing of my heart by writing of all that had led up to it.

The world has gone on spinning along its predestined route like some great top humming its way through space, carrying with it that load of mystery and marvel which we call life ; spinning and humming just as it has been doing through æons of time, always with the same speed and the same buzz, while we have opened our eyes and shut them and opened them again and wondered. Two little glimpses at the pulsing and throbbing of a little balance in the machinery of the universe ; and we rub our eyes and wonder.

Once more I look back, this time from a place farther along the track of time. For since the day when, rich with the gold brought from the pyramid built above the slaughtered ogre of Australian pre-historic life, I pined and

86

longed and fretted for the lonely bush, I have
been once more to the secret, desert-surrounded
range ; have seen once more the remnant of a
people who lived in power and splendour while
yet the Alps lay fathoms deep beneath a sea
that now no longer rolls; and have learned
that which for ever has dispelled my faith in
my own power for good or ill, save when
guided and controlled by the pre-ordered
destiny of fate.

It was upon the anniversary of my first
return to England that, in order to battle
with the persistent longing to journey again
to Australia and look upon the terrible fascina-
tions of the Yellow Queen once more, I wrote
down the story of my first experiences within
her territory. For a brief while I had relief,
but only for a brief while. Then the longing
came afresh upon me in a constant fretful
anxiety to get away from all that which should
have pleased and charmed, and voyage away
to the rough and ready existence inseparable
from exploring among the deserts of Central
Australia.

It is unnecessary to enter into the full detail
of my struggle to retain what I felt I was
gradually losing, for although there was the
ever-present subtle influence urging me to leave

the remainder of the men on the lighter, while on the other side of the vessel the crew of the other lighter sought in a similar wailing song a stimulus for their labours.

The glare from the braziers tinted the hurrying, wailing, dust-grimed figures with bold glints of ruddy colour, as they worked amidst the clouds of coal dust, or trotted up and down the planks into the cold, brighter gleam of the electric light, varying their dismal chants occasionally with strange discordant shouts and ejaculations as one of their number did not move quickly enough, or was too energetic, for the steady trot on the planks, and so brought upon himself the anathemas of his fellows. They wore but scanty attire ; short fluttering shirts on their bodies, and over their heads, loosely wound strips of heavy cloth. The coal dust gathered on their raiment and sparkled in the varying lights, but threw the shade into a misty, weird, unsubstantial dimness. There was a suggestiveness of the unearthly in all they did, and as their sad, monotonous chant fell upon my ears, there came to me the picture of the pigmy hordes who swarmed from behind that mysterious rock in the distant desert range. Only that the Arabs were of a larger build, they might have passed for a kindred race, so imp-like and ghoulish did they look as they toiled and chanted—the remnant of an ancient race doing the menial work of the later conqueror. Throughout the night they worked with an untiring energy that was worthy a higher task, until the dawn came up, and in the grey mist they became still more of the ghoul and less of the man. Then I left them and retired to my cabin to get what sleep I could.

By midday we had taken in as much coal as we needed, and were able to let go the shore-lines and steam slowly into the canal. It was a hot day, fierce in sun-glare, and with a dry scorching wind blowing from over the stretches of Egyptian desert, which made the upper deck of the steamer a place to be avoided. My cabin was fortunately on the port or lee side of the ship, and as I had it entirely to myself, I found it more pleasant to remain in, revelling in the freedom of deshabille.

I was stretched out on my bunk, lazy and indifferent, when I heard the telegraph bell ring in the engine room and immediately afterwards the faint throb of the slowly revolving screw ceased. Then the stream of air which, while the vessel was moving, was directed into my cabin by the windsail of the porthole, ceased ; I raised myself on to my elbow and glanced out at the bank of the canal, and saw that we were stationary.

"Some vessel going to pass us, I suppose," I dreamily thought before I lay back again, in order to drift once more into the lazy indifference I had been in before the sound of the telegraph bell disturbed me. But the fascination of lethargy had departed, and in its place there had come a feverish restlessness. which annoyed while yet it mastered me. For some minutes I turned and twisted from side to side, striving to regain the comfortable ease of my former position. But my senses refused to slumber and my muscles seemed to have become suddenly galvanised as they twitched and quivered. Impatiently I swung myself out of bunk and stood on the floor of the cabin, and then, without a reason or a thought, I drew in the windsail from the porthole and put out my head instead.

Immediately below me the limpid waters of the canal, reflecting in perfection the clear faultless blue of the sky overhead, rippled from the side of the vessel away to the dull yellow mound of sand which formed the bank of the canal on the Asian side—scarcely twenty yards away. From thence the sandy desert stretched away in a monotonous waste of drear sombre yellow as far as I could see, until it reached and became lost in the faint blue haze of distance. Here and there the ground undulated, or rose into rugged barren ridges, upon the tops of which the sun glared and burned, and scorched into the eyes as they caught the reflection.

The porthole was only large enough to permit of my head passing through, and my body was invisible to me ; only the black side of the vessel appeared when I looked downwards towards where my feet were ; only the black side of the vessel and the limpid blue water of the canal, growing pale and green as it came against the ship's side.

As I gazed across the water and over the barren sandy waste beyond, a terror came upon me ; for it was as though I, the sentient, feeling being, saw, felt and knew while yet I had no sense-cognisance of either limbs or body. And a fear came upon me, a fear which was part of a horror and a terror of absolute negation and personal eradication ; such a fear as might come to a man when he has drawn in his last breath, and realises that he still lives and has his being, though his heart has ceased to beat, his lungs to breathe, and his brain to act. A feeling of being and yet not being ; a sense

the immeasurable area of space from whence I could look forward and backward ; forward through the mists of eternity ; backward through the æons of time. There was no limit as to the range of my vision ; no measurement as to the scope of my knowledge. The ages of the past, vague, shadowy and unsubstantial as the remnants of dispersing mists, were as close to me as the life of a second ago, or the intense mystery of the formless future. For an instant I wavered as to the direction in which I should turn the force of my newfound energies. Then a fancy passed through me, not in words, but in sense only, for until I recalled it later and clothed it in material thought, it was without words.

"Let the future wait ; the record is in the past," was the form the fancy took in words, and so I formed it and fashioned my demand upon the will and impulse of the moment.

"Let the past be clear," I cried mentally. "Let me know the bygone record."

At once before me there rolled, in tumultuous confusion, a mass of visionary scenes and panoramas of pomps and splendours, until my senses whirled into a dizziness. From out the tangled blur there rose one scene clear and individual, surpassing in its loveliness ; a scene of landscape rich in the modulated glories of colour and graceful outline. Stately white buildings glistened in the sunlight; majestic trees, smothered in blossoms of delicate tints, waved their branches in the air and spread abroad the sweet fragrance of their flowers; rich grasses clothed the ground, the deep green being picked out by a myriad of many-coloured blooms, while in the more sheltered spots there was the gleam of water and the delicate fronds of filmy ferns.

Towards one such spot I seemed to be rushing with tempestuous speed, and as I came to it I saw beyond it a long, white, low building, in the wall of which there were many small windows. From one of them I saw the face of a girl looking towards me, a face that was as familiar to me as my own and one which set all my being vibrating with rapturous elation. I strove to reach out my arms towards it, but they were powerless; only could I look into the eyes that were turned towards mine and strain, in an agony of remorse, to get nearer.

Then, from somewhere in that shadowy land of beauty, there came a low, soft, wailing voice and I heard, in an unknown language, a sentence that I have never forgotten:

" Naggah, naggah, oom-moo-hah."

The agony of remorse was intensified a hundred-fold as I heard the words ; for it seemed to me that I both knew and understood them, and yet could not grasp their meaning. All my energies went out in the struggle, and with a wrench and a crash I came to myself, with my head hanging out of the cabin porthole and my eyes straining to get a last glimpse of another face, the face of a girl, which was looking towards me from out of the porthole of a passing steamer.

The vessel passed on its journey and out of my range of vision, the last thing I saw being that girlish face, before I drew in my head and stood, quivering and shaking, on the floor of my state-room.

Presently I heard the bell in the engine-room ring again, and a few moments later the steamer trembled as the screw began to revolve ; but I scarcely heeded it ; my mind was full of that visioned face, and my brain kept on repeating the words, " Naggah, naggah, oom-moo-hah."

For the remainder of the day the vision of that face and the echo of the unintelligible words haunted me, and made me even more pre-occupied and reserved than I had been since we started. With the restless anxiety which had preceded my departure and the subsequent placid content of mind when I was at last on board ship journeying to the south, I had paid but slight heed to my fellow-passengers. The simple interchange of ordinary everyday salutions and opinions were all that passed between me and them up to the day when I had gazed out over the Asian desert into the mysteries of time ; after that experience even this slight intercourse ceased on my part, and in lonely, silent brooding I lived through the days that had yet to elapse before we reached Australian waters. My fellow-voyagers possibly regarded me as a monomaniac of some description, for once the doctor of the ship came to me and spent some time with me, his manner and his conversation alike convincing me that he was striving to gauge my mental condition. I trust he was satisfied. Any way he did not repeat the experiment, and for the remainder of the voyage I was allowed to enjoy my solitary musings undisturbed.

As we neared the Australian coast, the restlessness which had preceded my departure from England, and which had slumbered during the voyage, came upon me again and I used to pace the deck with quick rapid strides, sniffing at the salt sea air in the hopes of distinguishing

the scent of the gums.   When we were a day's
journey from Albany, the wind was blowing
strongly from the direction where the great
Southern Land lay shrouded in its forest garb.
There must have been a big bush fire somewhere on the coast, for the smell of the gumtree
smoke was borne on the breeze, and a thin blue
haze hung along the horizon.   It was early in
the morning when I smelled it first.   As soon
as the dawn had come I was on the deck with
a longing in my heart that I might catch a
glimpse of the melancholy-hued coast, and as
I emerged from the companion on to the deck
my face caught the breeze and my nostrils
inhaled the faint pungency of the wind-blown
smoke.

I sprang to the side and held my face up to
the breeze, drawing in great sniffs of the
aromatic perfume, sweeter to me than the most
delicate essence made by man.   It was the old,
old smell that I had learned to dread so much
in the days when Smiles and I did battle against
the fires on Curriewildie Station, and strove to
save Mrs. Halliday's property from destruction.
Then we used to curse it when it reached us
on the soft bush breezes ; now I turned to it
and blessed it, aye, and worshipped it, and I
felt my heart grow light and my blood leap

as I caught it, for it spoke to me of home, and the home life, free and open, of the glorious unfettered bush. And even as I revelled in it, there came in to my mind another memory, and I clutched at the rail of the bulwarks; for it was not the hard dog's life we had had at Curriewildie in the last few months of our stay that the scent alone brought back to me. With a rush and a staggering distinctness my brain remembered—the girl's face in the steamer porthole and the unknown cry I had heard.

The men of the watch came round to wash down the decks, and I returned to my cabin and stood with my face at the open port, so that I could still breathe in the scent of the burning bush, while I tried to get some intelligible reason out of the tangled confusion which filled my mind. It was, however, a waste of effort, for the best I could do was only to separate my emotions into the conflicting combination of pleasure and sorrow, pleasure at the recognition of familiar tokens, and sorrow I knew not for what, save that the face I had seen on the steamer we had passed in the Suez Canal was in some way connected with it.

worse than invest a few thousands in such land, I was thinking, when I heard a quick step behind me, and a well-remembered voice exclaim :

"At last you have come. I had almost grown hopeless."

I turned towards the speaker and cried out in my surprise, for at my side stood the Hatter, gaunt, grey, and haggard.

"Great heavens," I cried. "What is the matter ?"

His magnificent physique was gone, and in its place he was thin, almost to emaciation, and there was an ugly stoop in his shoulders. His face had lost the bronze hue of health and was pallid, while his one-time raven hair was more than streaked with grey, and his eyes gleamed with an unhealthy light where formerly they had sparkled with a happy intelligence.

"Nothing—now you are here," he answered. "We'll start at once."

There was a feverish impatience in the man's voice and manner which I did not like.

"Start for where ?" I asked.

"To my place away back," he replied, nodding his head in the direction of the town.

"But all my traps are on board. I was going on to Adelaide before I landed, and only came ashore here for a stroll," I said.

" You're not going back on me now, are you ? " he asked quickly.

I only looked at him for answer, and he wrung my hand.

" God forgive me for doubting you," he went on ; " but I am tortured to death. Come to my humpy and we'll discuss it."

" First I shall have to get my luggage ashore," I answered. " Unless you care to come on to Adelaide ? "

" No," he replied shortly.

" Then I'll get my things on the wharf and go right along with you," I said.

He would not come on board with me, and I had some bother before I could get all my belongings put over the side into a shore boat. But at last I managed it, and went off the steamer without a soul bidding me good-bye. I fancy they were rather pleased than otherwise at getting rid of the "mad Australian," as I heard some of them term me once.

As soon as I was on the wharf I found the Hatter waiting for me with a dray.

" You'll have to pay for it," he said. " I'm stony broke ; but we cannot hump all this swag twenty miles through the bush, so I hired this dray in your name."

" What is there at the humpy ? " I asked.

"Nothing," he replied. "Don't I tell you I'm stony broke?"

"No horses or——"

"Nothing," he interrupted. "I took the land up—it's only sixty acres—but there's nothing on it save a few wallaby. I'm out of stores."

There was no need to inquire further; I knew from bygone experience all that he would have said if I questioned him for a day; so I climbed up into the dray, where my luggage was, and we started off for the township. At the first store we stopped, and I got down and went inside. The storekeeper glanced at my clothes and my fresh complexion, and I saw that he sized me up as a raw "new chum," and, consequently, a fair mark for a deal. When I gave my order he was rather taken aback, and executed it without even an argument as to the wisdom of my choice in the matter of the articles purchased. I laid in enough to last the two of us for a month, and when it was all on the dray we had a very fair load, especially as we had to ride in it as well.

"We had better get a couple of horses," I said. "There's more than enough on board without us, and we shall want them later."

"This is good enough," the Hatter said abruptly.

But I was disposed to argue the point with him, when he cut me short by remarking, "Do you want the whole township at our heels? Because you'll have it if you buy much more. They'll think we've struck gold somewhere near my humpy."

The warning came too late, for although we started away at once, we had not gone a mile before a couple of horsemen caught us up and travelled with us. We tried to shake them off by making a camp a good two hours before sunset, but they joined us, and we could not, by the rule of the road, refuse them a share of our fire and "tucker," particularly as they had none of the latter with them.

They were a decent pair of fellows, a little down on their luck, and terribly anxious to know whether there was any chance of their standing in with us in our find. It was useless our saying there was no find in the case; they said that the storekeeper was sure there was by the stores we had bought, and so he had put them up on horses on the understanding that they were to give him a third of anything that came of it. We had a lot of yarning before we learned as much as that, for both of them were smart chaps, and did not give their game away until they judged us to be as square as they were. They were mates who had come over from Queensland to make their pile in the Westralian rush, and had nearly made their graves instead.

"We'll give you the straight tip about it," the Hatter remarked, when they had told us about the storekeeper's dodge. "You've been square with us and we'll be the same with you. This is an old mate of mine," he continued, indicating me. "Some time ago he struck it rich and went home for a spell, but like many another he longed for a sniff of a campfire smoke and a taste of billy tea. So he came back. I struck it too, but dropped it, and was in Albany stony broke when I wandered to the wharf to see the mail boat come in, and on my way I met my old mate. I explained matters to him and he elected to come and spend a time at my humpy in the ranges and brought his own stores with him. And that's gospel ; so you can ride back in the morning or come on, if you like, and see my camp."

"You've a lay on somewhere," one of them remarked.

"Perhaps we have and perhaps we hav'n't," answered the Hatter. "Any way, we're not going there now, and when we do go you don't come, if you still stick to that storekeeper game."

"We're not very keen on that," the man answered, "provided the other is all right."

The Hatter remained silent for a time and I watched him closely. He evidently had something in his mind and as we had not as yet had time to discuss matters I was in the dark as to his motives, so I held my peace, knowing from experience that he was quite able to conduct the affair, whatever it was, to our best interests by himself.

"Then I'll tell you," he said presently. "My mate and I are going to my humpy, which is in the ranges, and there we shall stay a couple of weeks or maybe a month. You can go back and tell your storekeeper where we have gone and cry off the job, and then, in a fortnight's time, if you're on, you can come and pay us a visit, and we'll see what is in the wind then. Only you'll have to keep it a dead secret till we meet again."

They fell in with the proposal, and by the time we went to sleep it was arranged that they should accompany us as far as the humpy and then return to Albany, taking the empty dray with them.

By daylight the following morning we were on the road again and journeyed steadily until we arrived at the selection the Hatter had taken up in a small narrow valley between two steep ridges in the range, and upon which he had built his rough slab hut. We unloaded the dray and got all the stores and my baggage inside before our new friends left us on their return trip.

"Mind you, we're dealing square," the Hatter said at parting. "You keep it dark and get back in two weeks' time and you won't be sorry for it."

When they had gone out of sight I turned to him.

"What's your idea?" I asked.

He laughed as he answered :

"They helped us to get the stores in and they've saved us a journey with the dray, and after all, we may want a couple more with us when we start, and both those are good-hearted chaps. Any way, we score so far and at no cost to ourselves."

"I don't see why we should——" I began.

"No, my lad, I have not had time to spin my yarn yet. Wait till you hear that. You'll understand better then," he said, interrupting me.

CHAPTER X.

THE HATTER'S YARN.

WE had finished our evening meal and sat, one on either side of the wide open chimney up which the flames from the burning logs flared and danced. There was light enough for us to see the smoke from our pipes, and while the Hatter fulfilled his promise and told me all that had happened to him since he disappeared that night in Adelaide, I sat quiet, smoking and listening.

"I did not care to tell you about it at first," he said. "It seemed too ridiculous for me to believe, let alone any one else. But it mastered me; it mastered me."

He sat silent for a few minutes, gazing at the fire, and I watched him, noting how he had changed from the first evening I had scrutinised him by the firelight—that evening so long ago, as it seemed, when we had given one another our pledge to be mates to the end.

"Yes, it mastered me," he continued. "I tried to banish it from my mind but I could not; the look in that woman's eyes when she bade me hasten to her and liberate her from the horrors of her doom, has haunted me ever since—and I must go back."

Again he paused, and I let him rest without interruption.

"I meant to have gone with you; to have seen the old world again and tried to forget, in the pleasures of a re-awakened memory, the miseries of the past. But at that last dinner we had, the emotion I had been stemming back flowed over my barrier of self-control and swept me away in a stream, which whirled me round like a straw until it landed me here—here, penniless and hopeless."

His voice wailed with the last words and I reached out my hand and touched his.

"No, not now," I said quietly.

"No, not now," he answered dreamily, and then, as if bestirring himself, he went on with more vivacity in his voice, "You see, I forgot about the money. When you had gone I remembered that I could not at once start back for the land of her captivity, because I was without the means even to purchase a pair of blankets. But I had a desire driving me on, and I wandered over to Westralia again and struck a lucky spot, making enough to set me on my feet in a couple of months. I kept on until I had a fair amount in cash, and then I laid my plans. It was quite possible to miss the route the first time, so I decided to be prepared for a failure. I came down here from the goldfields and took up this patch of land and built this humpy. In one corner of it I constructed a little hiding place, which I will show you to-morrow, for the storing of all my surplus cash and some other things I wanted to have handy. I reckoned that if I never came back no one would find them, and that is the very end I wanted while you were not here. But I did come back."

" You have not started yet," I interrupted.

" Quite right," he answered. " I'm inclined to wander a bit, in the telling of this yarn, so keep me to it. I planted what I did not want, and then, having fitted myself out with a couple or so of horses, and stores enough to last me for three months, I started."

" My idea was to get away steadily towards the north-east until I struck somewhere about the place where I left you in charge of the camels when we came across that dray track leading to Coolgardie. I followed the scheme

8

out until I had travelled a good three days' journey beyond where I fancied I ought to have picked up some guiding point, but without discovering any. So I struck more easterly and soon got into desert country with longer and longer stages without water. My horses began to give over, for there was practically no feed for them, and when I did come to a patch I did not care to delay, so anxious was I to see that blue range showing on the horizon. It was madness to do it, but I did, and pressed on until one after the other my horses dropped in their tracks and I was left with only one, and he, poor brute, wasted to near a skeleton. I put on him as much as he could carry and trudged along beside him for another day, sure in my own mind that before the sun went down I should see the shade of the range on the skyline. But I did not, and that night saw the end of my last horse.

"In the dawning light I saw him lying on his side. I had about a pint of water in my water bag ; not enough to quench my own thirst, let alone revive him, so I left him where he lay and struggled on. My mind became a little confused then, and I lost count of things, until I came to my senses and found I was trying to squeeze another drop of moisture out of the dry canvas of the water bag, while the sun blazed down upon me and the horizon stretched all round me without a break or a rise. I fancy I must have fallen down, for it was dark when next I remember, and rain was falling. When daylight came I was wet through, and here and there in the hollows of the ground were little rain puddles which I drained before the sun came up, or it would soon have scorched them away. I managed to half fill my water bag, and then staggered along, fancying that I was still heading for the east, but in reality wandering aimlessly in every and any direction. At last I saw some trees in the distance and hurried towards them, finding a good-sized pool of water near them.

"After that everything is a blank, until I came to myself and found that I was lying under a tent. I learned afterwards that it was the camp of a prospecting party, one of the members of which had found me staggering blindly along, starving and jabbering incoherent nonsense. He took me to their camp and somehow or another they pulled me through. Then I wandered back here to refit."

He waited long enough to refill and light his pipe before he continued.

" The plant I had for my cash was all right

and I took a fairly long spell before I set about the fitting out of another expedition. I tried to persuade myself away from it time and again, but it was no good. The craze seemed to have sunk into my bones, and I only tortured myself when I tried to drive it out. The money I had left was not much more than enough to buy me horses and stores, and the little balance that was over I put in the hiding place again as a forlorn hope, in case I had to come back once more with another defeat behind me and the want of a spell in peace.

"Well, I did come back, sooner than I expected. Niggers settled me that time, by spearing my horses and nearly finishing me ; but I managed to get away somehow and reached a mining camp. I knew there was not enough cash here to set me up again, so I tried to make more. But it was no good. My luck had run clean out, and for months I could not even make enough to keep me in food. To improve matters I got the fever and so badly that, when I could move about again, I had not the strength to work. So I walked back to this humpy and lived on what I had hidden away.

"It was plain to me then, that I could not do the trip by myself, and I only knew of one

mate who would do it with me, and he was
the Lord knows where. The longing to go
was stronger than ever in my heart, and I sat
here yearning and yearning, and trying to send
out my soul to you, wherever you were, to tell
you to come. Then I spent my last shilling,
and ate my last bit of damper, and walked in
to Albany to face the end—when I met you.

"And that's my yarn," he added, after a few
minutes' silence. "If you had not come I fancy
it is all there ever would have been to tell,
for I was hopeless and heart-broken. But you
have put new life into me, and I only want
to be off again."

"You want a month's rest and a good course
of feeding before we start," I replied. "It's
no use starting on that trip unless we are prepared to do a good deal of hard work."

"That is so," he said. "And besides, we
must wait for those other two chaps. We can
do with their help; at least you can, because——"

"Because what?" I asked as he stopped.

"Well, perhaps you have not thought about
it, but when we reach there, your idea, I take
it, is to come back with more gold."

"Of course it is," I said.

"Yes, but you see mine is not. This time

I stay there—with her—and you'll want some mates to travel back with."

"You never mean—— " I began.

"I must, I must," he cried, excitedly. "I can never leave her again. I cannot reach there by myself, but I am not going to prevent you from getting back home again when you have helped me to find the way. There's gold enough for you and them, and a dozen more if need be, and why should not you have it?"

The expression of his determination to remain, when he succeeded in reaching once more the scene of our previous adventures, did not surprise me. I felt it long before he said it, and in my mind there was an echo of the wish. I wanted to penetrate behind that mysterious sliding stone, which moved at the sound of a voice, like the ancient doorway of the robbers' cave in the nursery story of Ali Baba. I wanted to see what there was at the back of it, and in that weird silent range, and I wanted to learn something more about the pigmy race that obeyed so implicitly the slightest sign of the awful creature with whom the Hatter was enamoured. More than that, there was an impulse within me, which almost suggested more than a passing interest on my part with the Yellow Woman herself, in spite of the terror with which she had inspired me when I first beheld her.

"I also wish to stay," I said quietly.

The Hatter swung round upon me with an ugly gleam in his eyes.

"You? Why should you stay? What is she to you?" he cried.

"She? Do you mean Tor Ymmothe?" I asked, in an unconcerned voice.

"Who else should I mean?" he replied abruptly.

I sat without replying for a minute or so, and then I said quietly:

"I want to see what there is behind that stone. I want to see where all that gold came from. There is a great and wonderful mystery in it all, and I want to clear the whole thing up before I come back."

"You will carry your life in your hands," he remarked.

"I have done that before," I answered. "The gain is worth the risk, and if we get into the stronghold or whatever it is, I reckon we can get out again."

"I shall never come out again," he said, with deep solemnity in his voice. "My life only has one aim now to keep it going, and that is to be with her. Once that is accomplished I care for nothing.   But it is different with you."

"You remember our compact?" I said. "We were to be mates to the end.   Do you want to go back on that now?"

He did not answer for a time, but sat still, staring at the fire.

"No, I do not want to go back on it," he answered at length.   "But things have changed since then.   I had a power over you then.   I have none now.   All I can do now is to urge you not to come with me farther than that pile of gold."

"And all that I can say is that I am determined to go with you behind that barrier as you are to go yourself.   I believe it was for that I returned, so do not try any longer to dissuade me from it, for I am absolutely determined."

He smoked on in silence, and I continued:

"My plan is very simple.   We will stay where we are for a time, and, while you are getting up your strength, you can teach me that jargon they speak over there, so that I can understand all that goes on if we ever do manage to reach the range again.   For the rest, we will consider the advisibility of taking those other two with us when they return here. For my own part, I do not fancy we shall ever see them again.

" Oh, yes, we shall," he said. " They will come back safe enough."

" Then we will discuss the matter further when they do. For the present let us camp for the night."

CHAPTER XI.

GUMTREE PHILOSOPHY.

THE following morning I awakened with the dawn, and, slipping out so as not to disturb the still slumbering Hatter, I went to the door of the humpy and watched the sun rays struggling through the morning mist which hung over the gumtrees in the vicinity. The tops of the ridges round about the place were already lit up with faint, rosy hues, and overhead the sky was of that wonderfully clear blue only seen when the sun rises on an Australian morning. The bush birds were chirping and twittering, and a gentle, cool breeze fanned my cheeks, and brought to my nostrils the peculiar scent of the eucalypt. I expanded my chest to breathe in the delicious air, and felt my pulses tingle and my blood rush through my veins. What was London, with all its joys and attractions that it offers so lavishly to a man of wealth, compared with this sublime delight

122

of breathing in the scented air of this dear sunlit southern land ?

I walked from the door to where a fallen log lay on the ground, and sat upon its bulky form and watched, as I had often watched before in the bygone days of station toil, the glow of sunshine spread over the country. It was difficult to imagine that only a few weeks ago I was in a city where such a sunrise was unknown, and where a glimpse of such a sky would have thrown the population into ecstasies. And yet I had voyaged half round the world to see it, and for no better reason than to——

" Doing a think ? "

I turned, startled at the voice and saw the Hatter standing just behind me.

" I fancied you were still asleep," I said.

" What, when the sun is up ? I'm too old a bushman for that. The first gleam of it always wakes me just as thoroughly as an alarm gong," he answered. "And I did not sleep very well last night," he went on. " I was thinking and I want to tell you at once. I'm glad you are coming with me into this unknown land."

He held out his hand to me and I grasped it warmly.

"You're a true mate, Dick, true all through," he said. "Don't let us say any more about it. The thing's settled now and I'll teach you Pitchorie and show you my plant."

"But there is nothing in it, you say," I replied.

"Oh yes, there is," he said. "Do you remember what I told you about myself?"

"I do," I answered.

"Well, it was not very clear, was it? Just a brief, vague outline. But since then I have written it all down in full, and that story is what I have in my secret dungeon cell," he added with a laugh.

"It is my whole history," he went on, his voice growing serious as he proceeded. "I do not expect ever to come back, but you may, and I want you to do something with it. I do not want you to touch it until you know for certain that I am no more. Then I wish you to return here, open that nook, read the paper which is in it and act as you please. That is all. If you don't care for the business, say so ; if you do, then just give me your word to that effect, and that you will not attempt to learn the story until I am gone."

"You wish me to promise ? " I asked.

"I should like you to," he answered.

" Then I give you my promise to carry out your wishes if I can, though I do not expect there will be any necessity," I replied.

" Thank you, Dick," he said as he held out his hand, which I clasped. " Now let us say no more about it and I will reveal the secret chamber," he added, with another laugh.

We returned to the hut and he pointed out two slabs, one on the northern and one on the western wall, and in each of which a brass hook was driven.

"Now you take that spade, and when you have drawn a line from one slab to the other, draw another one from that line, at right angles to it, up into that corner," and he indicated where the two walls met. " Then dig where the second line starts and go down two feet."

The floor of the hut was, as it usually is with rough-built bush humpies, the plain earth, and when I had made the lines he suggested I dug. At about two feet the spade struck a hard surface, and, clearing away the debris I discovered that the obstruction was a flat piece of stone.

" Lift it up," he exclaimed.

I did so, and found that it formed the top of a small square space which was carefully built up with flat stones. In the centre of the space a block of stone had been placed on several small pieces, and upon the block there was a package rolled up in waterproof cloth.

"That's the paper," he said, pointing to it.

"All right," I answered, and I replaced the flat stone on the top and filled in the hole I had dug, carefully smoothing away all sign of the lines I had traced on the surface.

"You've got it," the Hatter said when I had finished. "It's a good place, isn't it?"

"I think I had better leave all my papers there when we start," I answered. "No one will ever find them if we do not return."

"Oh, you'll come back," he remarked. "I am sure of that, and now, till we start, let us leave the subject alone."

There was a nervous anxiety in his voice and manner, so I fell in with him and carefully avoided any reference to the matter afterwards. The study of the Pitchorie tongue occupied my attention instead, and kept it fully engaged too, for of all the extraordinary combinations of sounds that man ever adopted as a means of conveying his thoughts to another, commend me to Pitchorie. To impart all its peculiarities to me occupied the Hatter very much more than the fortnight which was to elapse before the two men, who had followed us from Albany, were due to return.

I was not surprised when they did not appear to time, and told my companion that there was no longer any chance of their coming near us again. But he would not agree with my view and insisted that they would return later. In the meantime we struggled with the Pitchorie tongue,—the one to impart, the other to acquire. The steady occupation of the Hatter's mind, combined with the rest and the constant dieting I insisted on his following, had an excellent effect upon him, and I was glad to observe how every day he showed unmistakable signs of the return of his former strength and physique.

Another fortnight passed and I was sufficiently advanced in the Pitchorie tongue to carry on a conversation with the Hatter, if one can speak of a conversation in connection with a language which conveyed a greater amount of information by the omission of words than by their use.

It was the great stumbling block in my road to proficiency and fluency, this practice of omission ; but the Hatter was loud in its praises and maintained that it was, to him, evidence of the vast antiquity of the tongue, and of the tremendous heights of mental culture to which the race that once spoke it had attained.

"Do you mean to contend," I said one day to him, "that there was ever a race which was on a higher plane of civilisation and culture than our own?"

"Not only do I mean to contend it," he exclaimed, "I firmly believe it, and this tongue, spoken by an-out-of-the world remnant of humanity, as the tribe which inhabits the Pitchorie district may be termed, is to me a convincing proof of my contention."

I laughed scornfully in reply.

"Now, see here," he went on, speaking with some of his old warmth; "don't you make the big mistake that many people make. Our civilisation may be the best that we know of historically, but history does not represent everything that has ever occurred in this world. The Alps and the Himalayas are very high mountains as things go nowadays, but once they were below the sea and, when they were, other places which are now down were up. Just bear in mind that we know of grander mountain chains, of more tremendous pinnacles, and greater precipices rising from the bed of the ocean and yet beneath its surface, than anything that exists above its level. There is a sudden drop of five miles in the depth of the Pacific not one hundred miles from land, but you cannot show me a mountain peak which rises sheer five miles above the sea level to-day."

"But what has that got to do——" I began.

"What has that got to do with our civilisation? Is that what you are going to ask? Well, just wait a moment and I will come to that," he interrupted quickly. "We may fairly reason that, in ages far remote from the present, the earth's surface was very different from what it is to-day. We know the plants and animals that lived on it were different, and, if the plants and animals, why not the distribution of land and water? Our land at the present time is all moving, either up or down. Once Australia was divided into two parts by a sea which rolled where now South Australia exists. We know that, as absolutely as we can know anything by reason and deduction, for the eastern flora is distinct from the western flora, and they blend towards the middle, where there is any growth at all on the dry sandy desert which lies between them, and where the lakes are mostly salt,—that is, filled with sea water left by the tides millions of years ago when the land slowly rose above

9

the surface.   I don't want to go down to abyssmal depths for my illustrations, but if such changes have taken place in land, in animals, and in plants, why not in man also during the time he has been on the earth ?   How do we know that he was not, in the past, more highly civilised and cultured than we are to-day ? How do we know that we are only stumbling along the path he passed over millions of years ago ? ''

" But surely," I exclaimed, " surely you will not say that there has been a greater race and a greater civilisation than we have ? ''

" Why not ? " he answered.   " Just think a moment.   When Pompeii was overwhelmed with an eruption of Vesuvius, it was obliterated for centuries.   But we have evidences here in Australia of volcanoes, now extinct, which were fifty times as big as Vesuvius ; and tokens of earthquakes and cataclysms that pass the com-prehension of man to grasp.   Now supposing that such volcanoes suddenly burst forth in Europe and America in this year, flooding all the country with streams of lava hundreds of feet thick and keeping up an incessant can-nonade of earthquakes and convulsions.   Just imagine that as occurring for only one single month, and where would your great civilisation be ? Your cities, London in its millions, New York in its power, and all the rest of them, would be tumbling, crumbling heaps of ruins. And the people ? What would they do ? What would become of them ? Paralyse your trade for one month ; suspend your manufactures, stop your communication and spread over humanity the pall, the awful, terrifying pall of seismic eruption, and where would your civilisation be? But let that warfare of the elements run on for a generation—and more than a generation passed while the Alps were rearing their heads to their present altitude— and where is your world ? All the boasted triumphs of your age are forgotten. Those of your people who are not dead from fear or starvation, are babbling maniacs, terror-stricken and degraded to a herd of savages, struggling in the first rudimentary stages of the fight for physical existence. And all because the earth for what, in its life history, is but a brief moment, shakes and stretches itself and turns itself upon its heel. Oh, boastful, egotistical, blind-eyed man ! How cheap is your wisdom ; how insignificant your power ! "

There was a fine impressiveness about the Hatter when he let himself go like that on any subject. On our previous journey he had often poured forth, by the hour together, his views on Australia and its original inhabitants; but I was too dense or too indifferent then to pay very much heed to him. My one great hope on that journey had been to get rich. Well, I had got rich, and gone to the place where of all others in the world riches can command the greatest return, and had turned away from it all to come back again to the lonely, sad-hued bush and the thoughts that are possible under its spell.

I had often in my sojourn in London recalled the Hatter's orations, and as my mind became expanded under the influence of my surroundings, I regretted more and more my folly in not having paid closer attention to what he had to say, especially on the aborigines. I knew he had had a vast experience with them in all parts of the continent, and I was sure he also had that power of thought which unfortunately does not always accompany the men whose personal contact with the natives is their only reason for the claim they set up, as being the sole authority upon all things aboriginal. I wanted to hear him talk on the subject again, so I adopted the trick of opposing him, knowing that he would at once launch forth in his efforts to show me my errors.

"All that may be," I said. "But it does not explain any of the habits of the aboriginals."

He looked at me critically for a few moments.

"That is just what it does do," he said, at length. "It explains their habits as nothing else can do. Take, for example, their restless, nomadic life. Assuming that once before, in the long long ago, man lived on the earth's surface for a couple of thousand years, during which the world was free from any terrible convulsions of nature. It would be absolutely impossible that he should not rise in the scale of civilisation ; the common experience of the race during that two thousand years must have put the general intelligence higher at the end than it was at the beginning. Now, Britain two thousand years ago was little more than one of the larger Pacific islands is to-day, as regards the condition of its inhabitants. The early people of our race were tattooed, or stained, which is very much the same thing ; their weapons were the primitive bow, arrow, and spear, and they worshipped awe-inspiring deities, whom they sought to propitiate by human sacrifices. But at present they, or their descendants, are the highest civilised nation on the earth. In the last century they have made more progress in the acquisition of common experience [which is only another term for civilisation] than in the preceding ten. That is the result of a prolonged period of peace ; I mean peace so far as the natural forces are concerned.

"Occasionally there have been outbursts here and there. Krakatoa went down in a night, and a few hundred thousand people with it— only they happened to belong to one of the so-called inferior races, and we, of the ruling white caste, were not affected by the loss and, therefore paid scarcely any attention to it, beyond noting the fact that the eruption or convulsion was a magnificent pyrotechnic dis- play. In Japan, which I believe is a doomed remnant of a bygone continent, these occurrences are so frequent that they are scarcely noticed, and it wants a tremendous commotion to make a stir there. But it is within a hundred miles of the Japanese coast that the huge pit I mentioned as existing in the floor of the ocean has been found. Suppose the precipitous sides of that pit caved in ! Just fancy the displace- ment of water alone which would result, and the tidal wave which would sweep over the adjacent islands, even supposing that they did not also go down in the general collapse, and then say what the mental condition of the survivors would be. Do you imagine for one moment that any ordinary number of human beings could experience such a catastrophe as that and still retain all their up-to-date, civilised notions?"

"I do not see why they should not," I said, as he paused, evidently for my reply.

"Well, let me try and show you," he continued. "Your ordinary, up-to-date, civilised being would be somewhat upset, would he not?"

"I should imagine so," I assented.

"And assuming that the affair occurred in the night, he would be very glad to see daylight again?"

"Certainly," I said.

"But, however upset he might be, he would still be liable to experience hunger in due course, and have a desire to satisfy it?"

"Quite so," I agreed.

"Then how is he going to do it? Suppose such an occurrence took place in Europe, and Britain was affected. The ordinary citizen who survived would probably want a fire in the morning to warm himself, but he would have no matches and no coal. He would grow hungry, but there would be no shops open where he could buy the necessaries of life. There might be a few sheep, and he might by chance kill one; he might also manage to make a fire at which to cook part of it. But there might also be several other ordinary citizens who were hungry and cold. Now, would he share with them, or would he try to keep what he had to himself?"

"I should say he would stick to it," I replied.

"Yes; and what would that mean? A fight, and a fight under the most bitter conditions; for it would be for life on both sides. Assuming that our first ordinary citizen wins and has his feast. He feels slightly more secure when his hunger is appeased—and he remembers the cost of his meal. He is a murderer. The continued teaching of religion, which has become almost a hereditary instinct with him, re-asserts itself after the preliminary rush of rage and passion. Perhaps the elements renew their combat, and he feels the earth tremble under his feet; the sky over his head grows black with thunder-clouds, and all the horrors of cataclysmal fury surround him. What would it mean to him, but the sign of the wrath of an outraged deity? What state would he be in after twenty-four hours of such an experience? As I said a little while ago, he would be a babbling maniac, terror-stricken and cowed ; trembling at every sound he heard, lest it should be the forerunner of more awful tragedies ; shivering with anguish at the approach of night, and crouching in abject fear through the hours of darkness, his mind becoming less and less able to work and reason, and only the animal part of him, his hunger, his thirst, and his other appetites, remaining. Place two such creatures, male and female, together. The production of offspring would be inevitable, but what sort would they be ? I tell you that if such a climax came down upon us now, in the midst of all our boasted civilisation and pride, we should be within a year, the parents of gibbering animals of less brain power than the apes. The flower of our cultured civilisation would wither in a night, and in the after struggle for existence, those of whom we now speak as being coarse and brutal would be the only ones to survive. And even they would go farther down the scale of human intelligence than they are at present."

"And the aborigines ; where do they come in ? " I asked.

"They are the descendants of a race that passed through some such ordeal as I have spoken of," he answered solemnly. "Other branches of the race escaped, probably to the

If you turn a leaf on a twig the wrong way, or reverse the twining swirl of a vine, we should not notice it. But the black would. He would know at once that it was out of place, and consequently untidy. Bend a grass blade down, and the black, seeing it, knows that it could not grow that way, and he at once recognises the fact that some one or some thing has been there and disturbed it. But the majority of our race have no patience to care about all this. They see that the blacks are not in the habit of viewing things as we view them, and at once say that they have no view at all. It is the old fable of the two men and the two-sided shield; it is not that they have no view, but that they view differently from us; and we, in our impatient presumption, call them fools and dullards."

"It is an audacious theory," I said, after awhile. "How did you reason it all out?"

"I did not reason it all; it came to me in glimpses and suggestions during my lonely wanderings, until I saw it in all its clearness, and understood. That is why I want to penetrate the mystery of that desert range and learn the secret of that woman's life. I believe the proof of my theory is there."

"But if you are not coming back, what good will it be to the world?" I asked.

He looked at me and smiled.

"What does it matter to the world?" he said dreamily. "They would grab the gold; but do you think they would understand the object lesson taught by the last vestige of Lemuria? If they did, the millennium would have come; for they would understand that knowledge, and not money, constitutes the only real wealth."

CHAPTER XII.

A FRESH INTEREST.

IT was a month after my arrival at the Hatter's selection—Wonga, as he called it—when one evening, just as we were having a last smoke before turning in, we heard a horse trot up to the hut, and a voice calling out a question whether there was any one inside.

We went to the door, and in the dim light could see a man getting off his horse. He came up to us and we at once recognised one of the two men who had followed us from Albany.

"I was afraid you had cleared," he said; "but Oates and me didn't know how to send you word."

"We had nearly given you up," I exclaimed.

"Well you see," he continued, "it was not all our fault. That storekeeper chap's a perfect dandy in his way, and would have it that we were trying some dodge on him. So we had to take on a job of fencing to show that we were in earnest when we said there was nothing in following you. But still he suspected us, and neither of us could get away without being tracked until yesterday. Then we heard of another contract that was open for fencing away back, and I set off, telling him that I was going out after it. Even then he set a chap to follow me, but I dodged him this afternoon, and as soon as it got dark I came on, trusting to my luck to find the humpy."

"You are going to camp here?" the Hatter asked.

"Of course I am," he answered.

"Then turn your horse into the paddock behind and come in," the Hatter said, and went inside, leaving me to show the man where the " paddock "—about an acre, roughly fenced— was situated. When we got inside the Hatter had a fire blazing up the chimney, and the billy on to boil.

As soon as we were comfortably seated the newcomer began :

"Oates, that's my mate, and as white a man as ever walked," he was saying, when the Hatter interrupted him.

"We didn't get as far as names the last time we met," he remarked. "But we'd better exchange now. This is Dick Halwood ; I'm

"That's so," I added.

"Then I will," Bill went on. "Though it isn't a pleasant yarn. My father had two sons and a daughter. I was the youngest. My sister was the eldest and she fell foul of a fellow, curse him, who was a rich and titled scoundrel. She was handsome, and he made love to her and married her. Then he played fast and loose and broke her heart, but not until he had inveigled the old man into endorsing some bills. He never attempted to meet them, but bolted, like the coward that he was, and his disappearance broke my sister's heart, as it ruined and killed my father and left my brother and myself beggars. That's the yarn. Short and unpleasant, like a donkey's gallop."

"And—you never heard of him again?" the Hatter asked.

"Heard of him? Not much. Sir Claude Digby, of Tollen Hall, Baronet, was not the man to face trouble," Bill said sneeringly. "He left that to us," he added, "and never even inquired after the poor little innocent who came into the world when her mother went out."

"A baby? Was there a baby?"

The Hatter's eyes glistened as he asked the question; but Bill could only stare at the fire.

"Of course there was, and Charlie and I gave up the last bit of our birthright so that she should not live to be a pauper. Her aunt, my father's sister, has brought her up. Charlie died, and I came out to this infernal country to make a fortune and buy back the old place— and became a bush fencer instead."

"But you'll make your fortune ; you'll buy back the old place yet," the Hatter exclaimed.

"How do you know?" Bill asked sharply, facing round.

"Because, Dick and I——well, I cannot speak for him yet, but I am on to take you and your mate with us, and if he agrees——"

He paused and looked at me with a mute appeal in his eyes.

"I'm agreed, after hearing that yarn," I said.

"Then we'll show you where there is enough gold to buy up the whole county of Suffolk and then you can cry quits with this—what's his name? Digby?"

"Yes, that *was* his name," Bill answered, still eyeing the Hatter.

"That water's about boiling," I said, as I rose and went over to the fire and lifted the billy on one side. "Pass over the tea, Hatter," I continued. I did not care for the turn matters had taken, and wanted to get the conversation away from the sombre subject of sorrow-laden pasts. In addition to which there was another thing which disconcerted me. The anxiety of the Hatter to hear Bill's story, and the way in which he had received it, made an ugly suspicion come to my mind. Was the man I had stood by, and who had stood by me, going to turn out to be nobody else than the unprincipled scoundrel who was the villain of Bill's short but dramatic story?

It was an ugly suspicion, but it would not leave me; and, while Bill was taking his meal, I kept covertly watching the Hatter. As I watched, my feeling of resentment and suspicion grew stronger and stronger against him. He had told me that he had inherited a proud family name, which he had dragged down to the gutter before he left England for Australia. I knew that in the floating population in the interior there is many a man who, under a rough nickname, hides a life's tragedy and a smirched escutcheon. So there was nothing in the fact that the Hatter desired to conceal his real identity; nothing, that is, to suggest that he and the villain of Bill's little drama were one and the same. But yet I believed it, and I could not bring myself to think otherwise. I felt repelled from him as the evening wore on, and I am afraid that the feeling was not too well disguised.

We had a brief discussion before turning in as to the course we were to adopt, and it was decided that Bill should go on as soon as daylight, and work back to his mate. Within the next fortnight they were both to return to the selection, and, in the meantime, we were to make all the arrangements for a start to our misty, visionary range, of which we only gave Bill the vaguest outline. He left us in the morning, and the Hatter and I were alone once more.

"Dick," he said, when Bill had ridden out of sight, "would you like to open that packet in the hole under the floor?"

"I have already told you that I should not do so except under the conditions you named," I answered somewhat stiffly.

"I know that; but you looked at me last night when Bill was spinning that yarn of his, in a way that made me suspect you fancied I was the man he referred to. If you like, you can open that packet now and read the whole story," he said.

"I don't go back on my word," I said, shortly; but, all the same, I was sorely tempted.

"Well, I am satisfied with it," he said, with

a sad tone in his voice. "I would rather take it than a good many other men's bond. And that is why I ask you now to do something more for me. I want you to take any share of gold there may be for me out of this trip, and deal with it as you think I would wish you to, after reading my history?"

"Half of what we got last time is yours and waiting for you," I said.

"No. I gave all that up. I did not know then that——well, you'll understand some day. We do not all do as we should in this world; there are stronger things than human will and intelligence. You will do as I ask?"

"I will do as you ask," I answered.

"And I know you will never go back on your mate, whatever he may have been," he said, in a sad, pathetic tone of voice, as he looked at me with a peculiar, soft light in his eyes; and into my heart there came a great pity for him. After all, I thought, if he were the man Bill had spoken of, what right had I to judge him? He had been a true and sterling mate to me; and if he had done wrong in the past, surely he had paid for it in the lonely, blank, dreary life he had lived since. I yielded to the impulse of the moment and held out my hand.

"I don't know who or what you are, Hatter," I exclaimed. "But we started on the password of 'mates to the end,' and I don't go back on my word."

He grasped my hand in silence, and stood with averted head, as though he did not wish me to see his face. When he turned it to me his eyes were luminous and moist, and his voice trembled as he said:

"Please God you will never regret giving one poor devil a leg up in his misery."

CHAPTER XIII.

THE START FOR THE DESERT RANGE.

ALTHOUGH I could not allow myself to go back upon my word with the Hatter, the ugly suspicion I had formed effectually prevented me from mentioning to him anything of the experience I had had in the Suez Canal. I had intended to tell him as soon as I arrived; but one thing after the other turned the conversation whenever I attempted to approach the subject, until it ceased to be uppermost in my memory. Then came the visit of Bill, and my suspicion that my mate was the man he had inveighed against so severely, and all desire on my part to confide my experience to him left me. As the weeks wore on after my arrival, the weird effect of the experience gradually left me; the constant effort to acquire a mastery over the involved intricacies of the Pitchorie tongue probably assisting in no small degree to diminish the keenness of the memory.

A few days after Bill had departed we fell

to discussing our plan of campaign. It did not take us very long to agree as to the course we were to adopt. Now that we knew all about Bill and his mate, we did not hesitate about trusting to them to carry out any arrangement we made with them; and, with that clear in our minds, we decided as follows :—

We were to purchase a team of at least ten camels, which, on the outward journey, were to be laden mostly with water ; for, with the experience we had already had of the arid country we should have to travel over, water was the greatest necessity. A camel apiece to carry us, as well as our stores and ammunition, would leave six to carry water ; and that, we considered, would be ample. When we arrived at the oasis, where the mighty pile of gold was waiting for us, we would unload our team of everything except provisions and water enough to last Bill and his mate until they reached fertile country again. Two camels and some stores we would retain for our own subsequent use, and the rest could be utilised for the transportation of as many gold bricks as we could load. Then Bill and his mate could start with the bullion, on the understanding that they were not to divulge from whence it came ; but that, when we joined them, if we ever did so, we were to have half the proceeds. We anticipated that, with such a fortune as even half that load would be, the two men would be more than satisfied, while Bill would be enabled to buy back his old home again. It was to him, therefore, that we decided to entrust the keeping of our share, which, if we did not appear to claim it within a period of five years, he was to divide between himself and his mate. When the two joined us a few days later, and we put our proposal before them, they both accepted all our conditions.

As regards the balance of our arrangements, they only affected the Hatter and myself, and were not therefore communicated to our new mates. We decided that, as soon as our companions started back and were out of sight, we, being well armed, would go to the rock and challenge, as Tor Ymmothe had told us. Then, if the rock moved and the passage were open to us, we would enter. After that—well, it was a matter of awaiting developments before we could arrange anything further.

"But supposing the rock does not move?" I said, when we were discussing it.

"There is no need to suppose that," the Hatter answered, as he looked at me and smiled. "I am certain that it will."

From discussing our plan of action we naturally drifted to the action itself, and the first thing that demanded our attention was the preparing for the expedition. After considerable discussion, we agreed that it would be better to carry out our arrangements gradually, so as to avoid the chance of creating in the township that suspicion which was bound to follow any lavish expenditure for stores and other necessaries.

There was a big station over the ranges, the Hatter told me, and it was arranged that I should go there on foot and purchase a couple of horses with what ready cash I had ; after which I would ride down to Albany and communicate with the Adelaide bank, on which I had a draft and instruct them to remit the amount to Albany. Then I would draw all the money out, and bring it on with me to Wonga, and, leaving a portion of it in the hole under the floor in case of a reverse, travel on with the rest towards the goldfields and buy camels ; the Hatter meanwhile remaining at the selection for Bill and Oates to arrive, when they were to start off and meet me at a point on the route.

The first part of the arrangement was easily carried out, and having bought my two horses, I rode back to Wonga and handed one of them over to the Hatter, while I rode on into Albany with the other. It took some time to get my draft business fixed up, and while I was waiting I bought an outfit of weapons and ammunition for myself. When the money was available, I drew it out and returned to Wonga, where I found that Bill and Oates had already arrived.

The Hatter told me that he had already explained our scheme to the other two, and they re-affirmed their complete acceptance of it. We modified it sufficiently to allow Bill to join me in the purchase of camels, etc., while Oates and the Hatter travelled together and purchased arms for themselves. My money I divided amongst the four of us, Bill and I taking the largest share for the purchase of our team, while a sum in gold, which I had brought specially for deposit in the hole under the floor, I kept to myself until the Hatter got the other two out of the way and enabled me to hide it. I opened the place and placed it on the stone alongside the waterproof-covered manuscript. I was sorely tempted to open it and glance at its contents, just to satisfy myself whether my suspicions were correct or otherwise ; but I fought against the inclination, and hastily covered up the hiding-place and obliterated all trace of the disturbed soil.

The next morning we separated, Bill and I to visit the fields and obtain our camels and necessaries; the Hatter and Oates to travel slowly along towards the north-east and work to and fro until we overtook them at an arranged spot.

It is scarcely necessary to go into that part of our expedition and detail our adventures; how we visited one field after the other, buying a camel here and another there, always having to fence with numerous inquisitive miners, who, finding the alleged glory of Westralia not so pronounced upon a close acquaintance, were anxious to throw everything they had to the winds, if they could have a chance of striking something solid. And they were all suspicious that we had a find somewhere about, and wanted to follow us and " chip in " with our luck. There was a good deal of interest in it while it lasted, though the memory of it is dwarfed into comparatively nothing by the exciting incidents and episodes which occurred to me soon after. We managed to obtain all that we desired, and, with our cavalcade, moved along slowly towards the spot where we had arranged to meet the other two. We found them camped beside the only waterhole there was for miles round, and just on the fringe of the desert land. We elected to spend a day or so in idleness before we began the difficult ride across the shimmering sands in search of the Bunyip's Pool.

During our spell we overhauled our outfit and distributed the loads amongst the camels, and as the water was good, we filled all the kegs we had brought to carry our supplies, while we had the chance. The Hatter and Oates had horses with them, and we decided to take them with us, for although they would make a certain demand upon the water, if the worst came to the worst, they would be available for food, should our supply of salt beef— not too lavish—run out.

The Hatter and I tried to locate the position of the range we wanted to reach, and with our memory of the route we had taken to and from the place, and the situation of Coolgardie in regard to where we were at the time, we determined that it ought to be about north-north-east from our starting place. We made a rough sketch of a map and calculated how many miles we had to journey, and how long our stores of food and water would last, and then we started away from the camp and were soon in country where the scanty dwarfed vegetation and the preponderance of sandstone boulders told us we were at all events heading towards the dry desert interior.

With our previous experience of the blacks we kept a sharp look out until we reached the open, barren, sandy wastes. Then we pushed on, feeling safe from any attacks of wandering tribes. For ten days we struggled along through the heat and glare of the sun-scorched sand, and on the eleventh day our eyes were gladdened with the sight, away on the horizon, of the blue line of a range. Since we left the camp we had not seen a single waterhole, and our stock was already getting low when we saw that sign on the horizon.

It was early in the day when we first sighted it, and the Hatter was wild with delight as soon as he caught a glimpse of it.

" It's your luck that has done it," he exclaimed to me. " I knew we could find it if you were with us."

" But it may not be the right one after all," I said.

" I would swear to it, even at this distance," he answered. " Come along, boys; there's a fortune for everybody who wants it there," he shouted, as he urged his wearied horse forward.

We pressed on, and as the outline grew clearer and clearer I shared the Hatter's sanguine views.

An hour from sunset we saw the dark green of the trees showing distinctly ; the horses and the camels must have caught the scent of the water, for they needed no urging on our part to hasten forward. Then the glow of the setting sun was reflected among the trees and, as on our first visit, we reached the wonderful oasis when it was lit up with the rich red light of the dying sun.

After the long, dreary stretch of dry, scorching sand, there was an inexpressible pleasure in standing once more on green verdure, and the four of us rolled with delight on the grass ; while our animals, having drunk their fill, cropped at it with their loads still on their backs.

We had struck the lagoon on the side farthest away from the spot where the pyramid had been built, and the quick setting of the sun did not enable us to see whether it was still there. The Hatter suggested making a big fire, so that we could see how to unload the animals and make a secure camp.

" Do you think it safe ? " I said to him quietly, for we had not told the others about the race of pigmies who lived behind the cliff.

" Pah ! They will not come out till we call," he answered.

I was sceptical, and carefully looked to the

firearms while the others made the fire. But my fears were groundless and the Hatter was right. A huge blazing fire was made, but no pigmy army appeared.

As the flames leaped up and illumined the scene, the Hatter gave a shout of joy.

"There, my boys, there," he cried, pointing across the water to where, amid the shelter of clustering vegetation, a yellow gleam appeared. "Look at that, for that's the gold. Look how it gleams in the firelight."

With one accord we all started towards it and stumbled over roots and branches in our haste to reach it. As if it could have moved after waiting for us so long !

It is impossible to describe the wild, almost hysterical joy of our two mates, when they realised the fact that it was all solid gold. They danced and leaped about, beside themselves with delight, and even the Hatter and I were more or less carried away. We ought to have been more careful, and have mounted guard against a surprise, but the idea never entered our heads, and Bill and Oates were for loading up the camels at once. The Hatter and I managed to drive into them the folly of such a plan, and at last we persuaded them that the best thing to do was to have a meal ;

II

though, when we sat round the fire discussing it one or the other of them would jump to his feet every now and again, and run over to the pyramid to make sure that it was really all gold, and still there.

I suppose I was the least enthusiastic of the four, the result of my previous visit having robbed me of the delight Bill and Oates felt at the sight of so much wealth. They were still talking of all the wonders that they would be able to accomplish when they reached home again, when I felt myself gradually getting sleepy ; so without disturbing their conversation I quietly rolled a blanket round me, and, stretching out by the fire, I dozed away into a deep and dreamless sleep.

When I awakened the sun was shining, the fire was out, and my three companions lay soundly sleeping around me, while the camels and horses were peacefully browsing round the edge of the lagoon.

CHAPTER XIV.

THE RESULT OF EXPLORATION.

As soon as I was awake I arose, and inspected on my own account the pyramid of gold, and wandered along the pathway of golden bricks, between many of which the grass was growing, up to the bare face of rock behind which so much mystery existed.

The water still trickled down from the heights above into the deep pool, from whence we had seen emerge that hideous monster, whose remains still slumbered beneath that magnificent tomb that the myriad of pigmies had raised. I stood and watched it as it fell in tinkling sounds, over the lip of the cliff. The volume did not appear to have changed in the slightest since the last time I had looked upon it; there was no evidence that the pool had overflowed, and the stoppage of the grass at the end of the desert was just as sudden and clean cut.

I turned towards the rocky wall and examined it closely and carefully for some sign or token to guide me into finding where that hidden portal existed ; but all the face was smooth and unbroken, and I could find nothing which in any way could be regarded as a break or a crevice.

I applied my ear to the wall and listened attentively, but caught no sound and was in the act of removing my head when I glanced upward. Above my head I saw that a line ran across the face of the rock about ten feet from the ground.

I leaped back and looked, and now that I had discovered where to look, I wondered that I had not noticed the mark before. I could distinctly trace the line and saw that it was some six feet long and a good ten feet from the ground. From either end other lines, uneven and irregular, rose straight up to about twenty feet when they converged together until they met and formed a pointed arch. In tracing them my eyes also caught sight of something else, and that was a narrow ledge, which sloped up near the point where the water fell over, and which apparently went down to the foot of the wall some distance away.

Fired by my discovery, I hastened along the wall until I came to the edge of the water. A narrow ledge ran along and under the fall, and without stopping I hurried along it, pressing close against the rock so as to avoid slipping off into the water. I succeeded in reaching the other side where I found the vegetation growing thick and rank, and in order to examine the rock more closely, I shinned up a small thin sapling which grew close to it. When I had gained a point above the top of the undergrowth, I glanced towards the face of the cliff and saw that, a little farther on, the ledge I had noticed descended rapidly to the ground. I slipped down again and pushed my way rapidly through the bushes until I came to the place where the ledge was level with my waist.

It was barely two feet wide and sloped in towards the rock, rising in a steep grade to the top of the waterfall. I scrambled up on to it and, on my hands and knees, climbed slowly upwards. I was soon above the tops of the trees and could look out over them across the barren stretch of yellow sand, away to the horizon, where the desert merged into the blue mist of the sky. A little farther on and I was just below the jet of water and, looking carefully upwards, I saw that there was another ledge above me. I hastened along until my head was above it and then I saw that which made me start so violently that I almost lost my balance and nearly fell into the great deep pool below.

What I had taken to be another ledge was in reality the summit of a wall of some twelve feet in thickness and as my head rose above it and I was able to look over it, I saw, stretching away for at least a hundred yards, an expanse of rippling, sunlit water. Beyond the water there rose another rocky wall which I did little more than glance at, for a light breeze was blowing, and as my eyes caught the first glimpse of the ripples coming towards me, I started, the unexpected view impressing me with the idea that they were huge waves rolling down to overwhelm me. Fortunately my hands were tightly gripping the edge of the parapet, or I should have crashed down to destruction below. As it was, I could barely keep my balance and scrambled up on to the wall and lay there panting and trembling with the effort I had made.

When I had recovered my breath I looked around, and understood the mystery of the jet of water which spurted out from the face of the cliff and fell into the pool at its base. A channel had been cut through the solid rock up to within a foot of the edge, and the water of the lake flowed through it and then through a hole which had been pierced in the remaining foot of rock below the water's level. My eyes followed the causeway upon which I was resting, to where it swept round in a bold curve away towards the face of rock on the other side. I saw that it sloped up on one side to the summit of the next face, and as my glance travelled across that, I noticed a long thin silver streak standing out clear against the dark background of the rock. I was on my feet, intending to hasten round and satisfy myself whether the distant cliff was yet another retaining wall of a reservoir, when my ears caught the sound of a coo-ee away down below among the trees.

In my excitement I had forgotten all about my companions. The shouts were continued and I crept back to the edge of the cliff and looked over. They were evidently alarmed at my absence, for I could see them running hither and thither as they looked among the trees for me, and I could hear their coo-ees and their shouting of my name.

Lying flat on the top of the cliff, I put my head over the edge and gave a long loud coo-ee. They all heard me and looked up, but could not distinguish me, until I waved my hat, and I could then see them gesticulating and waving for me to come down.

I was about to do so when I heard a curious grating sound below me, and glancing down, I saw a slab of the wall at the place I had noticed the crevices, slowly fall outwards. I shouted out and looked towards the three; but they had also seen the rock moving, and I saw them run to the camp and come back a moment later with their rifles in their hands. The top of the slab of stone by that time was a foot away from the face of the cliff and I, clutching my revolver which I fortunately had in my belt, lay and watched it moving, with a breathless fascination.

Slowly it lowered, and from my position I could see that it was apparently working on a hinge; though how it was prevented from falling out at once I could not grasp. As it stood out from the wall I tried to peer into the black hollow space behind it, but I was too high to command any view of what there was beyond. It continued its slow descent until it stood out at right angles with the cliff; and I looked again at my comrades, who stood watching it as though they were spellbound. Then, from out of the space at the back of it, I saw a swarm of the pigmy people crowd out upon it, and the downward movement became quicker until the end of it touched the ground.

Those who were nearest at once jumped off, and then the whole swarm rushed forward looking, from where I lay, exactly like an army of ants streaming from a rift in an ant hill. The stone slab was covered with them and the ground grew black as they rushed on to the three men who stood without even raising their rifles.

In a moment, as it seemed to me, the swarm was upon them and over them and I saw the three borne down to the earth and held by the crowd of impish figures. I could not understand how it had happened, so quickly did the swarm do its work, but the three men were pulled over to the slab and dragged up its slope, exactly as if they were grains of wheat being carried off by ants. So fascinated was I that I could move neither hand nor foot as the extraordinary scene was being performed, and I only realised the full significance of it as I saw the stone slab rise rapidly, and, with a repetition of the grating sound, fit back into its place.

I cannot describe the feeling of hideous terror which then took possession of me. I dared not move from where I lay, not even to look behind me ; I could only lie and stare vacantly at the cliff where that great slab had grated back into its socket. I was torn with a thousand conflicting fears for my own and my comrades' safety until there came into my mind, with a flash, the recollection of how the Hatter and I had hidden ourselves from the vision of the pigmy army and its Yellow Queen on our previous visit.

At once I scrambled down the narrow ledge, and as soon as I reached the firm ground below I hastened to the spot where we had unloaded our team the night before. Then I remembered that we had no rope ladder in our kit, and, without thinking, I rushed about to try and find the stores we had discarded when we loaded up to our first team with gold. Covered and hidden by the undergrowth I found them un-injured by the exposure to that dry atmosphere. The ladder was where we had thrown it, and taking a coil of lanyard with me I sought and found the tree we had previously occupied. Fear and anxiety lent strength to my muscles ; and I was up in the branches, and had the lanyard thrown over one of the second tier, before I remembered that I had to go down again to fasten the end of it to the ladder. But it was long enough to hang over the branch while both ends reached the ground, and I came down the tree again and fetched the ladder, which I fastened to one end and pulled it up by hauling in the other. I hastily reclimbed the tree and secured the ladder to the branch, and, without a pause, worked with the energy of a fanatic until I had reconstructed a nest of blankets for myself, and had taken up all our arms and ammunition and enough food to last me for some days.

We had a couple of fowling pieces with us, as well as the rifles, and I carefully loaded them, as being more servicable against the pigmy swarms than the weapons which fired only single bullets; and, with them handy within my reach, I pulled the ladder up and lay down upon the blankets I had spread out on the branch, to watch and wait.

Throughout the day I stayed, straining my ears to catch a sound; but without any result, save weariness. The slab in the cliff did not move, and all that I could hear was the steady and persistent tinkle of the water, as it fell into the pool from the top of the cliff. The sun was going down towards the horizon, and I had seen and heard nothing which gave me any indication of the return of the pigmies, or the whereabouts of my comrades. I forced myself to eat some food, for which I had but little appetite, and then, when the sun had disappeared, I lay through the darkness of the night, filled with a terror and dismay which passes the power of language to describe. A horrible dread was in my mind, and I dared not look towards the spot where I knew the remains of that hideous monster we had slain lay resting beneath his pyramid of gold, nor towards the pool that shimmered through the darkness, lest my fancy should deceive me into believing that once more I saw the hideous form of the dead thing. The night seemed interminable to me, and I wonder now, looking back at it, how I came through it without a shattered mind. But at last a grey pallor spread over the sky, and I hailed it with feverish delight, for it was the token of the coming dawn.

When the sun mounted above the horizon, and I was able to look around and see everything as it had been when I last saw it the evening before, my mind was somewhat easier, and I ate ravenously, a circumstance which added to my confidence; for I reasoned that, while I could eat, I was not quite past hoping for. Still, I dared not descend from my lofty stronghold, but lay still throughout the day, anxiously wondering what had become of my comrades, and trying to formulate some plan by which I could help or rescue them. But everything I could think of seemed so utterly impracticable. I could not face those swarming myriads, even if I knew how to get that slab of stone out of its place; whereas, on the other hand, the Hatter, if he came before the Yellow Queen, would be able to hold his own with her, as he had done before. It was the latter idea which steadily gained upon me and kept me inactive; for I reasoned that it would be better for me to wait for developments, rather than rush into a course of action which might, after all, only make matters worse. So the day passed and night came on again, and once more I felt the horrible lonliness of my position.

While it was dark I could not sleep, but lay in an agony of suspense and dread, fearing at every moment, as I had feared the night before, that there would be some spectral appearance of the slaughtered horror. But none came, and when the sun rose once more I was exhausted in mind and body, and, having fed, dropped off from very fatigue into a deep, sound sleep.

The sky was red with the glow of the setting sun when I awakened and looked out away over the desert. Then I started up with a cry, for away in the distance I could see the dark line of the camels, walking as they only walk when they are driven, while a little on one side were the two horses with a man on each.

I looked down at the pyramid. It was disturbed, and the topmost layers of bricks were gone. Then the truth came upon me. While I slept, my comrades had been released or escaped ; they had sought for me, perhaps, but not being able to find me had given me up for lost, and had then loaded up the team and had started.

For a time I was beside myself with dismay, and know not what I did until I heard the warning, grating sound and found that I was stretched out on the ground at the foot of my tree. I sprang to the ladder and clambered up, drawing it after me when I had reached my nest. Then I lay still, terrified and un-nerved.

CHAPTER XV.

THE PIGMY SWARM AGAIN.

THE night was dark, and I could not even see the ground below me, as I lay with my eyes straining to pierce the gloom. But I could hear, and what I heard did not tend to soothe my nerves.

There was a soft pattering, first in the direction of the cliff, and then extending all over the place, and I knew that the myriad swarms of pigmies were running hither and thither among the trees. It occurred to me that they were seeking for me, and I lay still for fear that they should hear me if I only moved, and so discover my hiding-place.

The pattering of their feet, and the rustling of the leaves as they brushed past, continued for a time and then subsided, and the night was still and quiet again. I expected to hear the stone slab grate back into its place again, but it did not, and I was wondering whether it had done so without my hearing

175

and I, striving to cover her heart, fired too high and the bullet struck the knife, scarcely an inch away from her hand. Seeing that I had missed her, I caught up the shot-gun. A crowd of pigmies ran towards the knife where it had fallen, and stooped around it. With only a desire to kill in my mind I fired both barrels at them, the shot scattering them, while the shrieking and yelling broke out afresh.

I saw the woman standing still and erect, looking towards my nest, and, drawing my revolver, I snapped the trigger at her, the bullet striking the ground at her feet and splashing some soil over her. I was aiming more carefully at her heart when I heard the Hatter cry out :

"Steady, Dick ; steady. Don't shoot her. It's all right."

The woman turned round towards him and then looked up again in my direction.

" It's all right, old man," the Hatter continued, and to my intense surprise, I saw him rise from what I thought was about to be the altar of his sacrifice.

"For Heaven's sake, man, say what it all means," I shouted ; for with my nerves strung as they were I could think of nothing else to say.

The effect of my voice upon the Yellow Queen was magical.

She flung herself flat upon her face, and uttered a similar shriek to that which had so curdled my blood on the night we first saw her. It went through me with a thrill of horror, but it was evidently even more terrible to the swarm of shrivelled little ape-like creatures who were about her, for they moaned and whimpered in so agonised a fashion that I could scarcely keep from firing upon them, as one fires on wounded rats, to put them out of their misery.

The Hatter, standing by her prostrate figure, called out again.

"You've done it now, Dick; you're the King of Night after this. You must speak Pitchorie and tell her to go inside with all her people, and then I'll come and explain matters."

I acted on the suggestion. Anything was better than the anxious suspense I was in, and whether I made myself the King of Night, or any other mythical potentate, was a matter of indifference, so long as I could have a few words with a fellow-creature and obtain some idea of the mystery of all the recent events. I leaned forward and called out in the most impressive tone that I could adopt consistently with a correct pronunciation of that extra-ordinary tongue.

"Thou Queen of Lemuria, listen to me."

She sprang to her feet and stood with down drooped head and limply hanging arms.

"Retire with all your people behind the secret door in the rock, and there await our coming," I cried.

She turned and spoke to her swarms and then laid her arms upon the Hatter's shoulders.

"He is to stay," I yelled.

A sad wail broke from her lips.

"O King of Night, take not from me the light and glory of my life, even for one moment."

It struck me that the Hatter must have been making rapid progress with his *inamorata* to have made himself the light and glory of her life in a period of two days ; and a touch of sardonic humour came to me, giving my nerves a refreshing stimulus, and soothing my anxiety more than any thing else could have done.

"Did I not send him to you ?" I shouted.

"Yea, O Lord of Night," she answered submissively.

"Then obey, lest I take him away again for ever," I continued in an angry tone of voice.

She wanted no further inducement to depart, and, having marshalled her troops from the field, she flung her arms around the Hatter and then followed them.

We waited until the stone jarred back into its place.

"I'll just see if it's all clear," the Hatter said. "There's nothing like caution, now you're in it too."

I heard him walk away and I lay waiting until I heard his return.

"Here's the ladder," I said softly, when his footsteps sounded below me and I lowered the ladder down.

He climbed up slowly and when he was at the top and on to the bough, I pulled up the ladder also. Then he grasped me by the hand.

"For pity's sake, give me a smoke," he said. "I have not had one for days."

The mingled fear and distress I had experienced since I saw my comrades carried off, had actually driven all idea of smoking out of my head, but the mention of it by the Hatter brought the longing back to me with a rush.

"Neither have I," I exclaimed. "I was too scared."

I sought and found my pipe and some tobacco, and we shared it in turns. For the first few minutes we did not speak ; but at length, when it came to my turn to draw at it, the Hatter found his tongue.

"This is a pretty muddle," he said. "I thought you were miles away with the others."

"And I thought you were," I exclaimed.

"Me ? Why I said I had come to stop," he answered,

"Yes, but I only saw the team away in the distance——"

"Only saw them in the distance? Why, how was that ? " he interrupted me to ask.

The shortest way to explain was to tell him all that had occurred since I saw him and the others seized, so I detailed it as well as I could recall it.

"Well, this business gets more strange at every turn," he said meditatively. "You will have to go through with it now, whatever it means."

"Of course I shall have to go through with it ; for I do not see how I am to walk over that desert by myself."

"And I cannot come with you," he said.

"But tell me all that has taken place," I exclaimed. "Why did you let them collar you ? Why did not you shoot ? "

"I did not want to, and the others were too

scared to do anything when they saw the stone falling and Tor Ymmothe standing in resplendent majesty towering over the hordes of animated shrivelled mummies that surrounded her."

"She did not come out," I said.

"No. She stood inside the opening like an enshrined saint. But, of course, you could not see her from where you were."

"Tell me the whole story. Begin at the beginning," I exclaimed.

"Well don't interrupt me and I will," he replied, and commenced a story to which I listened with rapt attention.

It appeared that the three of them, tired out with their exertions on the night of our arrival, slept very much sounder and longer than I did. Oates was the first to awaken, and noticing that I was not by the fire, he roused the others, fearing that something had happened to me. They coo-eed to me but receiving no reply, searched for me among the trees, shouting all the while. As they could find no trace of me nor obtain any answer, the Hatter feared that the pigmies had surprised me and carried me off, and began to tell the other two about the secret, mysterious opening in the rock. But they only laughed at him and he led them to the place, to show them where the pigmies had come from, when I caught sight of them. Oates and Bill still laughed at his story and started shouting again when they heard my answer, and were looking up at me and wondering how I had managed to scale the precipice when the stone began to move.

The pigmies, hearing the noise, had told their Queen, and she at once concluding that it was her promised love, prepared to greet him in due state. The moving stone turned the ridicule of Bill and Oates into alarm, and they ran for their rifles. But when they saw the stone fall and the stream of pigmies rush forth, while the Yellow Queen stood towering above them, with her phosphorescent skin gleaming against the black shadow behind her, with her mass of marvellous hair hanging round her and her arms extended, they were paralysed so completely that they could not even raise their weapons, let alone use them.

He denied that the pigmies captured them, all the same. They only carried them into the interior in state, though the Hatter admitted that the state was somewhat crude.

Once inside, the stone rose into its place again, and they found themselves in impenetrable darkness, the only glimmer of light being that shed by the phosphorescence of the Queen, a by no means soothing apparition to Bill and Oates.

The Hatter told them to keep cool ; that they were all right, and that he would guarantee their safety. Then he addressed Tor Ymmothe in the Pitchorie tongue. He told her that he had come in obedience to the orders of the King of Night, who had also sent the two others who were with him. He was to stay with her and break the spell of her doom, but the others were to return from whence they came, carrying with them, as a token to the King of Night, as many of the yellow bricks from the bunyip's tomb as they chose.

She listened to him in silence, but when he stopped she broke out into a fury of anger. She reviled him and the King of Night and vowed that they should all be devoured, for if only one remained the spell of the doom could not be broken, save by her surrender of him, and that she would not allow.

"I could not make out what she meant," the Hatter said. "Nor do I understand it now ; but she kept on repeating, over and over again, 'Who will wake her ? Who will wake her, if only one remains ?' So as I was in the dark and it looked rather bad for all of us, I played a bold stroke. 'Queen of Lemuria,'

I cried. 'Beware the King of Night. Until he sees the others depart he will be in anger.' But the only answer she would give was to repeat her query, 'Who will wake her? Who will wake her, if only one remains?'"

Having once assumed a threatening tone with her, he felt that it would be suicidal to change it. For himself, he said he did not care, but the lives of Oates and Bill, as well as mine, depended upon his persuading her that the others were to be allowed to go free. The more he threatened, however, the more determined she became in her assertion that none should go. At last he lost patience and shouting out in a loud tone, he ordered her and her tribe to leave them where they were, while he communed with the King of Night. She retorted by inviting him to commune with the King of Night while she was present, and was casting doubts on the genuineness either of himself or his potentate when an idea came to him upon which he acted.

He quickly asked Bill and Oates whether they had their revolvers with them, and as they had, he told them to be ready to fire one shot straight up over their heads when he gave the word.

"It was a mad, reckless thing to do," he

went on. "It might have brought down the roof on our heads or anything else, for we did not know what there was above us except darkness. However, we had to do it, so I told the Queen that unless she retired we would each of us send a message to our King, telling him of her rebellion, and I threatened her with the most terrible consequences if she were there when the reply came back. She answered us with one of those marrow-thrilling laughs of hers and I gave the word to fire.

"The flames from the barrels shot directly up over our heads, and to those who did not know what gunpowder meant, must have had a terrible effect. But the crashing of the bullets against the rock overhead and the spatter of flying chips and splashes consequent upon the bullets striking made the effect a hundred-fold more weird. In a wild, hideous chorus of shrieks and screams, the whole horde, headed by Tor Ymmothe, rushed away into the darkness and disappeared.

"We had a momentary glimpse of our surroundings when the pistols flashed. We seemed to be in a large low-roofed cavern, the floor of which rose up to the roof round the edges, like the inside of a saucer. We could see no opening, but we could see on

"But what does she mean by 'the other one'?" I asked.

"I don't know what she means; but I do know I'm nearly starving, especially now that I have had a smoke," he replied.

I passed him some food, mentally reviling myself that my selfish curiosity had not given him time to ask for it before.

"It ought to be dawning soon," I exclaimed, glancing towards the east which was growing grey.

"Then we had better have a brief camp, and discuss our future plans when we have rested," he replied.

CHAPTER XVI.

BEHIND THE BARRIER.

WHEN I awakened the sun was well up in the sky, but the Hatter, wrapped in his yellow robe, lay still sleeping. I crept over to his side and examined the quaint garment he was wearing.

It was a long loose cloak, more like a clergyman's surplice than a robe perhaps, and was made of a very fine metallic-looking thread closely woven. I took a piece between my fingers and examined it carefully, and while I was so doing he awakened.

"It's a queer looking garb, isn't it? I believe it is made of a wonderfully fine gold thread, judging by the weight of it," he said, when he saw what I was doing.

He had expressed the idea that was in my mind, and my curiosity to visit the interior of that strange stronghold was more than intensified. What further extraordinary things might we not discover about this marvellous race,

191

shrivelled up through the course of vast ages into vitalised mummies, but who once had developed their arts into such a state of perfection as to be able to weave a veritable cloth of gold ?

We examined the article carefully, but there was no suggestion of any ornamental pattern upon it ; the weaving was extremely close and the thread marvellously fine, so that the whole piece was just a gleaming sheet of fine-spun gold, woven into shape without   seam or a stitch that we could discover.

" Well, never mind the rag," the Hatter exclaimed. " Let us have some breakfast and a smoke."

We elected to descend from our nest, feeling secure against interruption from the pigmies ; so we went down to the spot where we had camped. We found that Bill and Oates had left nearly the whole of the provisions behind them, sacrificed doubtless to the greed of gold, and we made a sumptuous meal, after which we smoked awhile, the Hatter recovering his own pipe again.

" I've got a plan," he said, breaking a silence which had lasted some time. " I don't know if you'll care for it, but it is the only thing I can think of."

"Let me hear it," I answered. "It seems that I must stay here for a time any way, until something turns up."

"Yes, that's it. You cannot attempt to walk across that desert; at least, not yet. Besides which, I should like to know all about that saying of the Queen. So this is my plan. We will make everything secure here in case of necessity arising for us to need a place in which to stand a siege. Most of the stuff we will haul up into the tree, keeping enough down here to last us for a month or so. There's ample, what with the stores we left and what those other two discarded, to keep us going for half a year. When we have made our arrangements we will summon Tor Ymmothe to open the gate, and we will play out our little drama."

"That is all very well," I said. "But what is the little drama?"

"I am coming to that. I shall tell her that you have been sent by the King of Night in response to her request; that, as we are of a different race to her people, we must have our own food which the King of Night has also sent, and which her hordes will have to carry inside for us. Then——well, then we shall have to wait developments."

13

"But we must know something of what they are likely to be," I said. The programme as it stood might be all very well for him, if he wanted to stay inside that mysterious place for the rest of his life, but as I had no such ambition, I could not quite see where I came in.

"Yes, we must, somehow; though I don't see how we are going to do it."

"I have it," I exclaimed. "When we were here before, you made her explain to you all about herself. She did not go much into detail, certainly, but she gave a fair outline of events. Why not do that again? Why not tell her she is commanded by this interesting potentate to tell me all she knows?"

"It's a good idea," he said, after a few moments' thought. "I'll try it."

"Then there is another point. How long is it to last? When do we start back and how are we to go?" I asked.

"I never go back," he said gravely. "If you want to I will do all I can to assist you short of accompanying you; but I don't believe you will want to. I cannot tell you why I believe it, but I do. There is going to be some strange business come out of this."

"I don't mind a little experience inside there," I said, pointing towards the face of rock. "But I am not prepared to enter it for life. We can go in all right and try to learn something of the mystery of it all, and then I think we shall be better out of it, and among civilised people again. Besides, we have to return to join Bill and Oates, and get our share of the gold they took away."

"I never go back," he answered, as he looked at me with a strange smile on his face. "If you want to go, I should advise you to start now. You are outside the barrier and know that there is only the desert between you and settled country, though that in itself is a fairly difficult obstacle to get over. But once inside there, neither you nor I know how to get out again. If your mind is set on getting home again, go now, and leave me to face the Queen alone; it is useless your coming in with me, if you want to get away again."

"If we can get in, we can get out again," I exclaimed. "For the rest, my curiosity is aroused, and I want to know more about the mystery of the people and the place. While we stick together we need not fear, however many the pigmies may be, and I reckon none of them are bullet-proof."

"It's a very risky business for you," he said gravely. "I tell you candidly I do not believe there is any chance of your coming out when you are once inside."

"Oh, well," I said. "We can only know about that when we are . there. For the present there is nothing to be done but, as you say, wait developments. If the worst comes to the worst, I must make the best of a bad job, and at all events it will be an experience."

So we set to work, and stored most of the provisions up in the tree ; and while we were doing so I kept on telling the Hatter that, if the worst did come, I should look to him to stand by me, even to the point of accompanying me from the place.

We found that Bill and Oates had been terribly reckless with the stores ; for they had discarded so much that we feared whether they had taken enough with them to last them until they reached settled country again. As it was, we had even more than sufficient to last us for six months, and we stacked nearly three months' supply, for the pigmies to carry inside for us. At last, just at sundown, we had everything ready. I was for waiting until the following morning before challenging the gate, but the Hatter insisted upon doing so at once. After all, he said, it was no use wasting time over the matter, and I, having a good stock of cartridges and a couple of revolvers in my belt, felt fairly secure and self-reliant and agreed to face the unknown.

The red glow of the setting sun lit up the face of rock when we approached it. The Hatter shouted out the name of Tor Ymmothe three times, and then we saw the stone slowly move and heard the strange grating sound as it left the solid rock. I did not wonder that Bill and Oates had been scared at it, for it had a weird effect upon me, and I knew what was behind it; though, looking back at the experience now, it was a trivial affair compared with what followed during our stay in that most uncanny of uncanny places.

The stone slowly fell until it stood out at right angles from the face of the cliff, and I could see that behind it there was a great yawning, dark cavern. Then it was sufficiently down for me to see what the others had seen. Along what I may term the threshold of the cave there was a line of pigmy forms, their eyes shining like the eyes of cats, with the dark background behind them and the ruddy glare of the sun in front. But it was not alone their eyes that the ruddy glare illumined.

Standing well within the cave, I saw the majestically moulded form of the Yellow Queen, her golden-hued skin shining like polished metal where the sun rays touched her, and with her great eyes glistening like living lights. It was a sight which held me speechless and moveless, and I scarcely noticed how the stone had descended to the ground, and how the troops of pigmies were swarming over it and towards us. I was dumbly fascinated, but the spell was rudely broken. A score of brown, shrivelled hands were laid upon my legs and I was lifted from my feet and laid, as helpless as a child, upon the broad of my back, while all over my body I felt those tiny hands plucking and grasping me, and all round my face the wizened faces of the living dead creatures were pressed, as they strove to lift me from the ground.

A thrill of the most intense horror passed over me, and I swung myself round in an effort to fling them away from me. I might as well have tried to fling off a swarm of bees, for the tiny hands gripped like steel and held me, and, even as I struggled, I was subdued into passive inertia.

I was carried up the sloping stone and into the darkness of the cavern, and through it again into a place where the air was wonderfully cool and the light soft and dim. There I was laid down gently, and the pattering of little feet told me that those who had borne me so easily were leaving me. I turned on my elbow, and glanced behind me just in time to see the last of the figures disappearing through a small, dark hole; and before I could leap to my feet the hole had disappeared, and I was staring at an apparently unbroken wall of a dull yellow colour. I glanced around me and found that I was in a large circular room, with an arching roof high above me, through which a soft light streamed and filled the entire chamber. The walls were all of a dull yellow colour, and when I approached them I found that they were built of the same sort of bricks that had been used to build the tomb above the dead bunyip. The floor was of the same material and I gasped as I realised that I was in a veritable golden chamber, the value of which would be almost incalculable were it to be transported into one of the civilised centres of the world.

On the side of the room farthest from the point where I had seen the pigmies disappearing was a heap, which I at first thought was only a pile of loose particles of metal. I went over to it and found that it was a number of cushions made of the same class of fabric as the Hatter's robe.

I sat down on them and sank into a deliciously soft couch which yielded to my weight only to cling around me with a caressing touch, in comparison with which the softest eider-down would be hard and rough. It was so entrancingly enjoyable, especially after the hard couch of a bushman's experience, that I lay back at full length, revelling in the luxury, and forgetting for the moment that I was alone and heaven only knew where.

When I remembered that, the spell of the soft dreamy couch was forgotten and I sprang to my feet and shouted out the Hatter's name. My voice echoed in an unearthly way all round and round the room, and then went up into the lofty dome and came back to me again in strangely modulated tones that made my blood run cold, so human and yet so utterly unearthly were they.

I dashed round the room, hammering the walls with my fist and kicking with my boots, but only to find them everywhere hard, solid and immovable. In despair, I found myself again at the place where the golden cushions lay spread, and threw myself upon them in a paroxysm of fear that had come to me. I buried my face in their soft clinging embrace and lay in a stupor of fear and alarm.

How long I remained in that position I do not know, but I was aroused from it by hearing my name called, and, springing up, I saw the Hatter standing in the middle of the room.

"Where have you come from?" I cried, for my hurried glance round the walls showed no opening.

For answer he pointed down to the floor and then, with a laugh, came towards me.

"This is the rummiest place I ever was in," he exclaimed. "Talk about modern science; why, it is not within a mile of what these ancient Lemurians could do. Do you know what?"

"I know I'm caged up here like a convict, and can find neither door nor opening by which to get out," I replied sharply.

"Well, don't try up there," he said, pointing to the roof.

"How can I, when it is anything up to fifty feet over my head?"

"Do you know what is on the top of it?" he asked. "Do you know what makes this room so cool and the light so soft?"

"What is the use of asking me such insane questions? How am I to know anything, seeing that those infernal little imps carried me in here

loose robe of similar yellow fabric to the one he was wearing ; only this one was worked into a wonderful pattern of extraordinary hieroglyphics, the figures being raised and spun from deeper coloured thread than the cloth itself.

I took it from his hands and examined it.

" We will study it afterwards," he said. " Let us hear the story first ; then we shall probably be able to read the signs better."

" You mean these things ? " I asked, pointing to one of the figures that was uncommonly like an ordinary shovel, with a big snake loosely twining round the handle.

" That, and the others ; they are the same old marks," he added dreamily. Then, rousing himself, he exclaimed, " Come, put on the robe of state," and I slipped it over my shoulders.

It entirely enveloped me from the head to the ground. My arms found their way through two arm-holes into long hanging sleeves, and the Hatter drew my attention to a long pointed hood which hung down the back, and which, when pulled up, covered my head.

" Am I a clown at a circus, or a Chinese idol ? " I said, as I turned myself round.

" You would impress the people of London if they could only see you now," he replied. " Are you ready ? "

Without waiting for any answer, he kicked three times on the floor. There was a slight noise in the wall, and the apparently solid mass had opened, showing a long passage, lit with the same soft light, leading away through the wall.

He stepped forward and I followed him, trying to discover how I could draw my revolvers in case of need.

The passage was wide and lofty, and about twenty yards from the opening it curved and led into a room similar to the one we had just left. But in this a pile of cushions was in the centre upon a raised platform, a few small piles being scattered over the floor below the level of that on the platform.

On the floor, in strange contrast with their surroundings, stood our smoke-stained billy and tin pannikins, a lump of damper, and some salt beef.

"The sublime and the ridiculous," the Hatter exclaimed with a grim smile. "And yet that old billy could buy up all the rest, for they did not seem to know anything about tin in the days of old Lemuria."

I was about to answer when a part of the wall opposite to us opened, and, clad in gorgeous robe, more resplendent than either the Hatter's or mine, Tor Ymmothe walked into the chamber, and the two openings closed.

CHAPTER XVII.

THE CONQUEST OF THE QUEEN.

SHE stopped at the platform upon which the cushions were piled, and stood looking at me long and steadily. On her face there was a smile of fiendish cynicism, and her eyes took an expression of the most hideous cruelty and coldness, such as I have only seen equalled in those of a snake when it has struck its prey, and lies coiled round its victim, holding it in an embrace of merciless rigidity, gloating in its enjoyment of the gradually weakening death-struggles of the hapless creature. A cold thrill of horror passed over me as I met those eyes, and I felt my flesh quiver and my heart flutter, as a feeling of faintness came upon me. Instinctively I knew that I was being dominated by her, and my mind leaped in a spasm of fear as the figures of the gruesome pigmies floated through my brain, and I understood the meaning of the words she had used when she told us that she was doomed to live upon the sub-

206

stance of those around her. Even now she was drawing the vital forces of my being from me, and soon I should be as those wretched creatures were, if I did not resist and overcome the glamour of her eyes.

The thought steeled my mind and I strained every nerve to meet and return her gaze. It was a terrible effort on my part to look into those pale, luminous orbs with the phosphorescent flames flickering away within their lambent depths. I could not have stood it much longer, when she shifted her glance to the Hatter and said in a softened voice :

"He whom the King of Night has sent is strong of will ; surely he will succeed where others have failed."

The Hatter mumbled in reply, and I looked at him. His eyes had drooped before hers, and she held him helpless under the terrible fascination of her glance. This, then, was the reason of his anxiety to return to her dominion ; she had bewitched him on that eventful evening, when he appeared before her.

If he, the strong-willed man, who had so easily overcome my mental powers, fell so quickly under her thraldom, what chance should I have, I asked myself. The fear that followed the thought and the horrible possibility of defeat wrought my mind into a perfect fever of desperate resolve, and, with all my faculties roused and alert, I met her glance again with a fixed gaze and a fierce determination in my brain that, if I could not subdue, I would not be subdued.

I felt that she was exerting herself to break down my resistance, and that she was calling to her aid all the devilish tricks and subtleties of her black, magic arts. In my ignorance I knew not what to do to cope with them ; all that I could do was to set my teeth and clench my hands the while I held my mind in a fierce resolve that I would not yield, whatever forces and powers were brought against me. Suddenly, I know not how, I felt that I was gaining an ascendency ; her eyes drooped before mine once more, and then her head leaned forward and she raised her hands as though to shield her face.

"Hold up your head," I cried sharply ; and she did so, keeping her eyes, however, still cast down.

"You dare to pit your strength against mine," I exclaimed angrily. "Try it once more and I turn you into a dead thing, such as the bunyip is, who sleeps by the lagoon beneath the trees."

She sank forward and crept towards me on her hands and knees.

"Oh, thou, who art of almighty power," she said ; "take the place that you would grace so well and reign with me. We can dispose of this," and she extended a hand towards the Hatter.

"Speak such a tale again, and I let loose the waters above our heads," I cried, with more than simulated anger. It was maddening to think of all the time and money the Hatter had wasted for the sake of this cold-blooded monster, who now, because she had been able to subdue his will to hers, wanted to dispose of him and make way for another.

She looked up at my face, her eyes flickering and gleaming in a horribly repulsive manner. Then she leaped to her feet and stood towering over me, her face working and her hands clenched, but with her eyes always averted from the glance I steadily fixed upon her. It was a battle royal while it lasted, between the subtle forces of our natures. But I had already gained too much advantage over her for her efforts to set back my control, though I felt myself growing weaker and weaker under the strain of a contest I could only blindly realise. Perhaps she also understood that it was of no

14

terror was not unreal. " I will speak it, though it means the loss of my life and love."

She wailed out the last few words, and I heard the Hatter murmur under his breath, " Poor lonely devil."

She retired a few paces from us, and then turned and faced us with her hands clasped in front of her and her eyes hidden by her drooped eyelids.

" In the days ere the stranger came from afar and rebuked the king, my father, there was in a neighbouring land a prince's daughter, fair and lovely to behold. And the king, my father, whose will was law on the earth, in the air, and in the waters, and whose wishes were never disputed or gainsaid, saw her, and saw that she was beautiful.

"She, in the folly and conceit of her form and features, laughed when she heard of it, and spoke of the king, my father, who could never grow old, but was always in the heyday of youth, as of one who was ancient and decrepit. And my father, hearing of this, sent forth his embassies and had the girl brought before him and installed in his palace.

" Later, there came to them a daughter, more lovely than even the mother had been, and she was the joy and the flower in the life of the king,

my father. All the treasures of his kingdom
were for her ; all the beauties of the universe he
would have brought to her, had she asked for
them ; her word and her will were second only
to one other, and that one the king, my father.

" As she grew up, she grew more and more
beautiful ; and the king, my father, the mightiest
of all mighty monarchs, sought for a fitting
mate for her. Over the entire universe he sent
messengers and embassies, and many a visitor
came forward to claim her, even in the face of
the conditions imposed, which were acceptance
by her or death at the hands of the priests on
the sacred blood-red altar, which was never dry
through twice ten thousand years.

" In the first year many came, and many were
scorned by her and seized by the priests to be
laid upon that sacred altar, which gleamed with
the blood that dripped from their tortured flesh ;
and the youths and maidens who else would
have been the daily sacrifice, escaped with their
lives, and those who were yet to serve the ritual
of the priests clamoured for more suitors, so that
they too might escape the doom of sacrifice.

" But the fame of her coldness, and of the
thousands who had shed all their hearts' blood
upon the altar of the priests, spread over all the
earth ; and at last there came a time when no

more suitors came, and the priests clamoured that she herself would have to be handed over to them, so that the altar might be cleansed and made fit once more for the sacrificial youths and maidens. Then was the king, my father, sad in his heart ; but the priests were obdurate, and a fiat went forth that if, within the life of another moon, no suitor came, she, the joy and light of the earth would be yielded up, that her blood might moisten that holiest of altars.

"The king, my father, grieved and perplexed, called together all the wise men and women of the world and bade them prophesy. Many of them prophesied a suitor within the early days of the coming moon ; but no suitor came, and the blood of the false prophets was shed to keep wet the sacred altar until none would prophesy, and the king, my father, groaned in the affliction of his' mind.

"At this time there arose an old man, who came from afar and told how a suitor would come who would be the chosen of the fair daughter of the great king, but whom neither the king nor the priests would allow to wed her ; for the man would be a slave of the poorest class. Then would the priests exert their power, and on the altar would the blood of the accepted suitor flow, even as that of the rejected ones had flowed. But the maid would wed none other than the outcast slave she loved, and when his blood was spilt, her soul would meet his beyond the stars, while her body sank and slumbered till the sway of the king, my father, and the power of the priests, were dead, and the empire of Lemuria had shrunk to a forgotten dream.

"When the king, my father, heard the prophecy, he raged in his wrath, and the priests seized the aged prophet and carried him to the blood-stained altar and slew him upon it. But before another moon had risen there came to the palace gate a slave of the meanest class, clad in rags, who claimed the right of the maiden's choice, and her hand if she accepted. The priests sought that he should be given over to them at once, but the king, my father, refused until he had proved the truth of his words. Then was the fairest maid brought in, and she straightway turned to the ragged slave and, smiling upon him, took his hand and proclaimed him as her love.

"The king, my father, raved and stormed; the priests clamoured and threatened; but the pride of the universe laughed them all to scorn and swore she would wed none other than the lover she had chosen.

"All the great ones of the earth were called together to pronounce a judgment upon the slave, and they pronounced that he should be led away to the altar of the sacrifice. The priests seized upon him and dragged him from the presence of her who loved him, but before he could be taken he looked back on her and cried, 'Sleep, in the sleep of death, until I come to you, and say, "Death, O Death, thy reign is ended."'"

As she uttered the last words I leaped from the cushions, a flood of vivid emotions surging through my being; for the words she used were the words I had heard in the vision on the steamer in the Suez Canel.

She looked at me as I stood there, trembling in my excitement, and said again the words :

"Naggah, naggah, oom-moo-hah."

"She—this girl of whom you speak, where is she now?" I cried.

"She sleeps in the silent chamber, where the lamp burns that gives light to the palace, and which will burn until he who is to awaken her enters the chamber and calls upon her to awake. Then, either she awakens or he dies ; either I and my race are liberated from the doom that is upon us, or it extends to him who fruitless dares to challenge it."

"Lead me to the place where she is," I exclaimed, when I felt a hand upon my arm and, glancing round, I saw the Hatter standing beside me.

"Not now, Dick; wait awhile, until we can arrange for our escape," he said, in English.

"But I must go," I exclaimed impatiently.

"It may be only a trap," he whispered. "Just a trap to separate us. Don't leave me alone with her just yet," he added, with an appealing look in his eyes.

"You don't understand this. It is something I have not mentioned to you," I said.

"I know that," he answered. "You did not trust me after Bill came. Perhaps you were right; but now it is different. Our very lives depend upon you now. I dare not face her alone again. For God's sake save me from that."

"Are you ready?" Tor Ymmothe exclaimed, interrupting us.

"I will go to-morrow," I said.

"Send her away," the Hatter whispered. "I'll watch how she opens the wall."

"You must come now," she answered. "You must come now, or I will never show you the way."

"Obey my words," I shouted, "or I will

call down upon you the anger of him who sent me."

She covertly glanced at my face and then, turning away, walked to the wall. She leaned forward with her hands against it and stamped her foot three times on the floor, when a panel slid aside, leaving an open space leading into a passage. She passed through and the panel closed.

We both sprang towards the spot and tried to trace the panel; but in the dim, soft light we could not find a sign of where it began or ended.

"After a spell we will try that dodge," the Hatter said. "In the meantime, let us eat while we may."

CHAPTER XVIII.

A FLIGHT FOR LIFE.

IN spite of the peculiarity of our situation we had excellent appetites, although we had to content ourselves with what cold tea remained in the billy for liquid refreshment. Then we filled our pipes, and stretched out upon the luxurious cushions, wrapped in our eccentric-looking robes, in mind a couple of ordinary bushmen, but in appearance undeniable candidates for admission to the nearest lunatic asylum. While I had the opportunity, I arranged one of my revolvers, so that it would be ready for immediate service; the attitude of Tor Ymmothe not being conducive to trusting confidence on my part.

"You have saved my life and more than my life," the Hatter exclaimed suddenly.

"What do you mean?" I asked; for at the moment I was thinking whether I should fire on the Yellow Woman when next she appeared and trust to luck to solve the mystery of the sleeping girl and the queer cry that I had heard, or rely upon my newly discovered psychic powers to subjugate her to my will and learn all the secrets of the weird, unearthly place we were in.

" Just now," he continued.

" When she was in here, do you mean? Oh, you were only a little unnerved. I have the whip hand of her now, so we need not fear. Even if she does try any more of her infernal tricks, I reckon a revolver shot will put an end to them ; and it will hardly be murder to kill such a monster as she is," I said.

He shook his head and looked down with a terrible expression of despair on his face.

" Why did you come in? Why did not you go away? I warned you as much as I dared. We shall never get away now," he said slowly, with almost a whine in his voice.

" I came here to find out what things were, and I'm going to do it," I answered briskly. " If I cannot get away it will be a bad job, both for that Yellow Queen and her swarms, I can tell you."

" It's no good," he mumbled. " We are helpless now."

I tried to laugh at him, though to tell the truth I was far from feeling mirthful. He seemed so utterly depressed since he had commenced to speak.

"There's something you don't know," he went on. "I did not tell you before. Don't blame me. I could not. I shall not be able to do so soon, either. I feel it coming on again."

"Rouse yourself up, man," I exclaimed. "What is the good of all this silly nonsense?"

"It isn't nonsense, Dick; I wish it were," he answered. "Listen. I will tell you now. Quickly. Don't interrupt. When I joined you in the tree, after she had gone, I only told you part of what had happened. The three of us were not left together. I was taken away and brought in here. She came in and fixed me with those terrible eyes of hers until I felt them burning right into my being. I struggled against it at first, but I was powerless to resist; and soon I felt myself sinking under her control. Then she came towards me and took my hands in hers, and laughed that awful laugh of hers; and I felt my strength oozing out of my body. I knew that she was drawing out of me all that made me a sentient, strong, human being; and her eyes glistened and gleamed with ghoulish glee as she saw me shrink and shiver."

"Go on," I said, as he paused.

"At that moment I hated her, but I could do nothing but what she said. She told me that one was enough at a time, and that the others would be allowed to go, as many others had been allowed in the past, so that they would come back from the horrors of the desert, and she could then serve them, as she intended to serve me, at her leisure. When they had gone I was to be laid on the grave of the monster we had slaughtered, until she had drawn, atom by atom, the vital principles from my body, and I was reduced to a level with the other victims of her hideous life."

"Do you mean——" I began.

"All those shrivelled mummies were once vigorous men, like you and I. But she has sucked their life out of their bodies until they have become the wizened-up imps we know. Many of them may have come here as we came, in search of gold and wealth. How many bushmen have disappeared without leaving a trace behind them? Think of it. They may be among that swarm."

His eyes glistened horribly as he spoke, and I reached out and took him by the hand.

"Go on with your story," I said quietly. "Never mind the other part."

"I was to be one of them, and should have been by this time, perhaps, had you not been at hand to save me. You have gained what I have lost, and it is the only card to play against her now. And since then you have done it again. Here. Just now. For since we were carried into this infernal place, she has once more drawn my vitality out of my being and made me the slave of her will—till you broke through her spell—and here am I; my God, what a fool!"

He sprang to his feet and flung away the gleaming yellow robe he was wearing.

"Take it off!" he shouted. "I had to make you wear it so that you should become impregnated with its properties and yield yourself to her wretched wiles. Take it off; it is bewitched."

"Nonsense, man, nonsense," I exclaimed. "How can a robe like this influence me? Besides, these sleeves are handy to hide my revolvers, and I may want to use them on the lady before I am through."

He looked at me vacantly for a moment.

"It's no good, Dick, she will devour us," he said.

"Rouse up, man," I exclaimed. "What has come over you? You did not talk like——"

"I know," he said. "But that yellow crea-ture has paralysed me. I cannot resist."

"Listen to me," I said sternly, hoping to rouse him from the dangerous mental condition he was evidently drifting into. "You heard the words she said just now?"

He shuddered.

"Yes, I heard them," he said. "She said, 'I am coming now to devour you—both of you.'"

"Rubbish," I cried. "I mean, when she was telling us about the sleeping girl. Well, when I way on my way out here I heard those words in the Suez Canal, and saw—something I had never seen before."

"It's no good," he moaned, as he sank down into the cushions again. "We are lost. She will devour us. She is coming now."

I could see that he was terribly unnerved, and a fear that I had felt before returned to me. Was he going mad?

It was an ugly thought to have—ugly when it first came to me at Wonga, but a hundred times more ugly now; and I was trying to force it back when the wall opened and Tor Ymmothe stood before us.

The Hatter rose and walked towards her in a slouching, listless manner.

" ' And now for you ! ' she cried, as she stepped over him where
he lay."

[Page 225.

"Come back!" I shouted to him, gripping my revolver with the intention of shooting at her directly he moved from between us.

He paid no heed to me, and she laughed at me, showing her gleaming white teeth as she uttered her blood-curdling laugh.

"Hatter," I shouted; "stand aside, or I will shoot——"

I might as well have called to the wall, for he staggered over to her and rolled at her feet like an abject, cowering hound.

"And now for you," she cried, as she stepped over him where he lay; and I felt the hideous influence of those ghastly eyes upon me.

"Stop, or I will call the aid of him who sent me," I shouted.

Again she laughed as she approached me, with outstretched arms and blazing eyes; and I saw that all round the room the walls had opened in innumerable panels, and myriads of the pigmy forms were crowding through the openings.

I twisted my revolver from under my robe and fired, unable at the moment to know whether the barrel was pointing up or down. I heard the bullet crash over my head and knew that I had fired at the roof.

The flash of fire and the report of the shot

15

terrified the woman momentarily ; but it was not the effect of either that brought from her lips the hideous scream she uttered, and which found an echo from every pigmy as they went careering through the openings in the walls.

The splash of water on the floor beside me was the explanation. My shot had smashed through the dome of the roof and the water was flooding in upon us.

I leaped towards the spot where the Hatter lay, and dragged him along towards a doorway ; and even then the water was trickling over the floor from the column which descended from the roof.

"Hatter! Quick! Get up!" I shouted, striving to rouse him, when I saw Tor Ymmothe dart between me and the opening, her wealth of hair streaming out behind her as she fled.

The pigmies had disappeared and only she, the Hatter, and myself, remained in the chamber. In a moment it flashed into my mind what it would mean if she escaped, and I sprang after her. As I sped I saw the panels closing.

I just remember getting beside her and charging her with all my weight, sending her staggering on one side, and, unable to stop the impetus of my rush, I was through the opening just as the panel slipped into its place.

I found myself in a wide, lofty passage, the floor of which sloped upwards. It was this last fact which alone impressed me at the moment; for I was only conscious of the instinct of self-preservation, as I sped along the passage as fast as my legs would carry me. The robe inconvenienced me, but I would not stop to take it off, being satisfied to pull it up and twist it, as I ran, round my waist.

The passage turned and twisted, but I paid no heed to its course, so long as the floor continued to rise, until I saw in the dim light a flight of steps in front of me. I leaped up them two and three at a time, until I had exhausted my breath. Then I paused, gasping and panting, and with the perspiration streaming from every pore in my body. The light was gradually growing less as I ascended and, looking ahead, I saw the stairs vanish into a deep impenetrable gloom.

I stood where I was, listening intently. A faint sound came to me and as I strained my ears to catch it more distinctly, it was as if a gentle breeze were blowing; but besides the soft sound of the breeze, I heard the lip, lip of ripples of water. I knew not where the steps might lead me, nor what I might encounter in the darkness above me; but the sounds

I heard only had one significance to me and that was the steady pursuit of the water from the flooded room below. I turned again to the ascent and clambered and staggered up the steps.

Presently, through the gloom above me I saw a faint glimmer of light, such as might come from a starlit sky, and a fresh, gentle breeze fanned my cheek. I redoubled my efforts, and, in a few more steps, found myself standing on a small landing with the stairs going on above me, but at the side an open doorway, through which I could see the deep blue of the tropical sky studded over with its brilliant planets and stars.

I approached the doorway, seeing as I did so that the platform or landing upon which I stood terminated apparently at a dark, solid wall. I stepped forward, and found that the wall turned at right angles a little further ahead; and, continuing my way cautiously and slowly, I found myself at the end of the wall and the platform at the same time, and gazing upon a scene, the grandeur of which forced me to start backwards, and so escape a headlong plunge into the depths below.

A quick glance revealed to me where I was. Far below me there glistened in luminous phosphorescence, such as one sees on the ocean in tropical climes, the reservoir I had discovered when I scaled the cliff above the Bunyip's pool. I could trace the dark outline of the rocky wall which surrounded it ; and, away beyond that again, merging with the fainter hue of the horizon, I could see the flat desert, stretching away in its arid monotony.

Near at hand I could hear the sound of falling water, and I knew at once that I was standing somewhere on the face of the cliff I had seen across the surface of the reservoir, and down which I had traced the silver thread of a waterfall. I looked upward and saw the cliff still towering above me, and without hesitating further I returned to the steps, and resumed the ascent of them. They had hitherto risen steadily in one direction, so that, while the light lasted, one could look down to their commencement. But now they were in the form of a spiral, and I held the centre pillar with one hand while I felt the outer wall with the other.

I was now in impenetrable darkness, and no sound came to me save the soft hum of the breeze, and the tinkle of the falling water as I climbed up and up along what seemed to be a never ending ladder, until once more the glimmer of the starlit sky showed above me, and I emerged through another open doorway and stood on the summit of the second cliff.

On one side, away down below in the silent darkness, lay that lambent pool, while on the other side I gazed across a vast expanse of water rippling in the breeze, and flickering with a ghostly pallor of phosphorescence. The pathway on which I stood wound along in front of me, and, as I followed it with my eyes, I saw how it skirted the pool round to the other side where what appeared to be trees stood out against the skyline.

I decided to follow it; and, walking very cautiously, I went along it, with the waters of that great pool on the one hand, and on the other a sheer drop of some hundreds of feet. The pathway was some twenty feet wide and fairly smooth, and I went nearly half-way round before I stopped.

The exertion of climbing those steps was beginning to tell on my strength now that fear no longer spurred me on to escape from the overwhelming flood, and I halted for a brief rest at a point where the path widened into a plateau, some fifty feet across. A few boulder-like knobs stood out above the surface, and beside one of them I lay down.

The night was wonderfully silent, the soft breeze that had been blowing on the lower level not being apparent where I was lying. Only the lip, lip of the minute ripples came to my ears in a delicious monotony that acted upon my tired faculties so quickly that I was asleep before I realised that I was drowsy.

CHAPTER XIX.

A CRY FROM THE DARKNESS.

THE heat of the sun shining down upon me awakened me, and, as I sat up, I uttered an involuntary exclamation at the beauty of the scene before my eyes.

I was lying on what was evidently the rim of a huge rocky crater. It was filled almost to the brim with water, which caught the clear blue of the cloudless sky overhead and reflected it back in its full, rich intensity of colour, save where surface ripples were touched by the golden sunlight and flashed and glittered in streaks of liquid fire. The pathway along which I had wandered in the dark was the rim of the cup-shaped crater, not always so smooth as where I was, for some distance away and farther round, I saw a jagged broken wall rising into queer, fantastic shapes, which, in the darkness, I had mistaken for the loom of tree shadows. I looked away across the water to where the pathway appeared to run into a solid block of stone on the nearest side of which I could see, as a dark patch, the opening through which I had emerged.

Looking away from the water across the desert over which we had come, I could see it stretching away in its miles of glaring yellow sand, while immediately beneath me the lower reservoir, evidently the remains of another huge crater, glittered in similar blue and golden hues ; but I could see nothing of the trees that grew round the pool at its base. Looking in the opposite direction from the desert, I saw a mighty range of peaks and eminences, thrown together and jumbled about in as much confusion as if they had sprung up in a night and crowded and jostled one another in their hurry to climb up, so that none could rise without a kink or a twist in their form. The bright, clear, dry air brought them very close to me. The sun shone upon them and made them glow in rich pink hues where they caught the full glare ; but where fissures and gullies scored their sides, as well as on the slopes that were sheltered from the sun, shadows of purple-blue formed a wonderful colour contrast with the sunlit hues, and made the jagged, ragged forms marvellously soft and beautiful.

But nowhere was there any sign of life ; nowhere a suggestion of vegetation ; not even where the water rippled against the moistened rock was a patch of moss or lichen visible. All was dead and silent, and as I gazed upon the scene, so exalting in its beauty of colour and impressive in its wildness of form, the awfulness of desolation grew upon me and made me depressed and sad.

To help me to throw off the sombre feelings that were coming upon me, I renewed my walk round the crater, with the intention of making a closer examination of the fantastic shapes of the wall of rock which lay farther round. But as I approached I saw that the pathway suddenly turned in between two columnar blocks of stone. I hastened forward and found that it was as if the solid face of the rock had been cleft, so as to leave a narrow pathway in between.

I turned into this narrow alley way and walked along it. The walls on either side rose sheer up for some twenty feet, while the pathway between them, scarcely three feet wide, was smooth and sandy, so that my footsteps made little noise. The sun was not high enough to shine directly down between the two walls, and the air was cool and the light soft as I advanced. The passage sloped down for some distance, and then, branching off at a sharp angle, led up to another open doorway in the face of the rock.

Enough light came from behind me to enable me to see, as I peered into the opening, that the passage was roofed over, and that it widened out on the other side of the opening, while the floor sloped at a greater decline. Determining to follow it, I walked through the opening, and then, slowly downwards, along the passage. It soon changed from the straight, and twisted and turned, sometimes having a floor smooth and even, and at others rough and sloping. The light gradually decreased as I proceeded, the coolness of the atmosphere became more pronounced, and the silence more intense ; and yet the feeling of depression which had been upon me when I started, was gone, and in its place there had come an exhilarating excitement and a keen desire to press on.

The passage became so tortuous that I was turning at every three or four steps. Then it narrowed until my shoulders touched the sides as I walked, and the turnings were so sharp that I felt sure I should soon come to the end of it; when, having squeezed round one more than usually sharp turn, I found that I was standing just within a vast chamber, in the centre of which a mass of semi-transparent substance shone with a curious glow.

I hurried across to it and curiously examined

it. It was, to all appearances, a block of clear yellow quartz, through which a light radiated as though the sun were shining below it and through it. I walked round and round it, and clambered up on top of it, in the hopes that I should be able to peer down and understand whence the light came from. But I could see nothing more than the gleam through the yellow mass. I fancied that on one side of it the light was stronger than on the other ; and, looking up, I found that it was on the side opposite to where I had entered the chamber. Possibly, I thought, there is a continuation of the passage down at that end of the chamber, and I hastened over to the wall to examine it.

There was no continuation of the passage, but close to the ground I saw a small opening, and stooped down to examine it. As far as I could see, the opening seemed to run into the rock ; lying prone, I tried to wriggle into it. My shoulders pressed against the sides, and my chest and back touched the floor and roof, but my hands, which I had stretched out to the full extent of my arms in front of me, felt the walls trend away on either side. I gave a push with my feet to help me reach the wider portion. I was now in absolute darkness, and as I felt with my hands along the sides of the passage, I found what seemed to be a crevice running vertically on each wall. I bent my fingers over, and gave a vigorous pull. My body slid forward, and my arms reached out on either side into space. The floor seemed to glide from under me, and I flung my arms down in order to press them on the floor and stop my advance. They went out to their full reach without touching anything, and at the same moment the floor went from under me, and I felt I was falling. I clenched my hands, and set my teeth as I rushed through the air, nerving myself for the hideous smash I knew must come.

A plunge into ice-cold water was the last thing that I expected, and so I sank down and down before I recovered sufficiently from the shock to strike out for the surface. When at last I managed to get my head above the surface, I was almost breathless, and, weighted by the heavy clinging cloak that had become loosened as I fell, I could scarcely manage to keep myself afloat.

My sensations were horrible. All around me was absolutely dark; below me was a depth of water I knew not how profound; and the only sound was the echo of my own gasps for breath, and the splash of the water as I strove to swim. I had no means of ascertaining whether I was in a stream or still water; whether the pool was of large size, or only a flooded shaft. I struggled sturdily to keep myself a-float, thinking of little else till there came into my mind a hideous fear. What if, in the depths below me, there should be another monster such as the one we slew when first we came to the range? Why such an idea of all others should have come to me at that moment I do not know, but the effect of it upon my nerves was beyond description. Cold as the water was, my blood ran colder; a terror came upon me that, even as I floated, some such awful creature might be rising from below to seize me and drag me down; and I flung myself forward, floundering and splashing, and the echoes of the noise I made reverberated over my head and added to my fear. To go forward might mean only to rush into the clutches of an unseen foe; to wait where I was seemed to be courting the very end I wished to escape, and, in the frantic whirl and fury of my terror, I shouted for help where I knew no human being could hear me.

I cried out in one long wailing yell, and, as the sound left me, I moaned in the anguish of despair. For the cry echoed and rumbled through the darkness, and from a dozen points around me there came back my cry of " Help!" in every shade and intensity of hideous mockery. It travelled from side to side of that great immeasurable space, throbbing and fluttering in a myriad of whispered calls ; pulsating over my head ; floating away into some cavernous distance to come back with a jeer, and a mock-ing taunt, as though some envious sprite had caught it, and flung it back in a tone of malicious glee. The echoes were re-echoed and multiplied as they sped, until the articulate cry was lost in a confused babble of noise, which, to my straining nerves, was as a burst of revolting, fiendish laughter.

Then the sounds seemed to gather themselves together in the vault above my head, and rush away into the darkness, till they were only a faint tremor of vibration somewhere away in the depths of the night. They had almost ceased, when they seemed to be returning towards me, and I held my breath to listen. They grew louder and louder each moment, and a roar of sound came upon me, as though a thousand lusty voices were shouting and shrieking in hoarse derision from the depths of the impenetrable darkness.

I lay in the water, helpless and inert, as I

heard the sounds pass over and around me, and spread out again to die once more into whispers as though they were chasing one another through all the mysteries of that vast mountain cavern. Again they faded almost out of hearing before they came back in stronger intensity, and as they came nearer and nearer, my terror passed all control, and I made the hideousness still more awful as I shrieked and plunged in the frenzy of despair.

The sound of my voice seemed to meet the returning echoes and throw them into still wilder confusion, producing vibrations and tones before which my heart almost ceased to beat, as the fiendish crash and war of noise boomed and howled, surging from side to side in jarring eccentricities until I almost felt the water quiver. Then a mighty sound of rending filled the air, and a lurid flare of light formed a gleaming halo round a huge mass of rock, which I saw fall out from the space in front of me.

It fell with a tremendous splash, throwing the surface of the water into a rage of disturbance, which swept over me and hurled me about like a straw. A few seconds more of the unearthly rage of noise and I must have sunk beneath the flood, if only to escape from the pitiless tornado of terror that swept through my brain ; but when the water broke over me, I felt that I was fighting an element that at least I understood, and so I struggled against it, and kept myself afloat.

I saw that, where the mass of rock had fallen, an opening had been left, through which there came a blaze of light that lit up the space around me, and showed me, some thirty yards ahead, a floor of rock scarce a foot above the surface. I struck out for it with all the desperation of a drowning man, but before I could reach it, the return waves of the mighty splash came hissing and fuming from behind me, and, lifting me in their rush, hurled me into the second cave and threw me, bruised and exhausted, on the floor.

As the water flowed back again I lay like a log, and the little breath that was left in my body was almost expended as the flood washed over me, trundling me on the hard rock. I was more dead than alive when it had gone. I knew not where I was, save that I was on solid ground with a strange gleam of light around me, as I felt the last vestige of my strength leaving me, and I sank into a blank of unconsciousness.

CHAPTER XX.

THE LIVING DEAD.

WHEN I recovered my senses I was wet and cold, lying on the smooth floor of a large cavern. The interior was lit up with a bright clear light, so much like sunlight that I felt certain there must be some passage way leading from the cavern into the open air. The presence of the light, and the conviction in my mind that I should soon be able to get out of the mysterious passages and dark caverns into the day, revived my courage, and I was able to look around me and note the appearance of the place I had literally fallen into.

As I rose to my feet there was directly in front of me the wide jagged opening from whence the mass of rock had fallen when the echoes of my cry had come back magnified into a fury of sound. I stepped towards it and looked out upon the great pool of water beyond. The light from the cavern where I was, streamed out over it and revealed its motionless surface stretching far away into the mountain until it disappeared in the gloom and blackness of the distant shadow.

Overhead the roof sloped up from where I stood into a vast dome, the top of which I could not see, but beyond the light dimly revealed the other side descending to within some twenty feet of the water. It did not look so very far away from me as I stood gazing at it, for the rock swept round on either hand and joined it in almost a circle. I fancied I could throw a stone over to it, and picking up a small fragment of loose rock, I threw it with all my strength. It fell into the water with a hollow resounding splash very much less than half-way across, and the ripples that it caused caught the light and glittered as they swept over the black stillness of the pool.

As I watched them my attention was arrested by the echoes of the splash. It sounded all round the dome, travelling from place to place, as though it were bouncing round the rocky wall. Then it passed under the sloping roof beyond, and I heard it grow fainter and fainter in the distance until it was just a whisper of the original noise. But it did not cease. It seemed as though it had passed in a curving journey like a boomerang and turned when it reached the end of its course to return with magnified power, gaining strength at every repetition until it burst into the dome again with a roar as of a mighty billow crashing against a cliff.

The air trembled as it passed me, and died away behind me while I stood and wondered. There was a great mystery in front of me, some extraordinary natural formation which had the power of magnifying sound, and I wished for the moment that I had the ability and the knowledge necessary to understand it; but that was impossible, and I could only wonder then, as I wonder now, how such a marvel came about. I was tempted to fire my revolver and watch the effect of the explosion, but I had only a limited supply of cartridges and was not sure even whether they were not spoiled by the wet.

So I turned away from the dark gloom of the pool and the darker gloom of the cavernous tunnels and glanced round the place where I was standing.

It was a chamber which, with its smooth walls and level floor, suggested other than natural agencies in its construction. The roof was domed, but in a regular form and at either end of the wall, immediately opposite the opening on to the pool, there were unmistak-able doorways through which streamed the light which illumined the place.

I walked across to one and found that it led into a short passage-way, beyond which there seemed to be a large open space. Proceeding to the other I found a similar passage-way terminating in a similar open space, and I elected to follow along it. A few steps carried me through and into another vast chamber, in the centre of which there stood what at first sight appeared to be a mass of glowing quartz. Immediately over it, in the ceiling of the chamber, I saw another and similar mass and this I guessed to be the object which had so excited my curiosity when I passed from the narrow passage-way into the cavern, from whence I ultimately escaped by way of that terrible pool.

As I approached this extraordinarily luminous body, I noticed that there were similar masses at intervals round the walls of the chamber and my attention was more upon them than the one in the centre of the floor until I was close upon it. When I turned my eyes towards it, I stopped in my amazement, and stood staring at it.

In shape it was a cube, made of some transparent substance, and in the middle of it lay the form of a girl, while at each corner there was a radiant pyramid of luminous flame.

That was all which I was capable of observing at the moment, for directly I caught a glimpse of the girl's face my heart stood still, and I felt as though every nerve in my body had become numbed into inaction. I stood, scarcely breathing, with my eyes fixed by a strange fascination on the face, for it was the face I had seen looking out at me from the long, low, white building on the sunlit scene of my vision in the Suez Canal.

I know not how long I stood entranced, but dimly through my mind there flitted memories, sweet in their beauty, though too visionary to be more than passing phantasies. A curious sense of familiarity with my surroundings, and with the features of the girl within the crystal cube, and a half-formed feeling of having a previous knowledge of the whole scene, came to me. I knew not what was going to occur, to the extent of being able to definitely state in words ; but yet it was all familiar, and I felt I was waiting for that to occur which I knew would occur, and yet could not express.

As I stood, the light from the four pyramidal

flames grew dim to my sight, and over me there came a mist as of vapour. My eyes lost their power of vision for the solid material things before me, but acquired the power of looking through them upon other things which were ordinarily invisible. I saw around me and the crystal cube, the shadowy forms of scores of beings, whose eyes looked out from the vision-ary heads with a mute, but terrible appeal in their glances. I saw, within the dull opaque body within the cube, a luminous haze confined and imprisoned by the denser material around it, and I knew that it was seeking freedom, and that only I could give it the power to shake off the cloying bonds that held it. And I watched it as it fluttered and trembled in its efforts to seek its own way out, and knew that for centuries it had so fluttered and trembled, and would continue to do so for centuries more if I held aloof from helping it.

My vision, growing stronger, swept farther afield, and I looked through the dense rock around me, and I saw the plan of the mountain, and of the Lemurian palace within it, at a glance. I saw the chamber where the Hatter and I had been, filled with water, and I sought for the Hatter. At once I saw him, with Tor Ymmothe, toiling up a long flight of stairs which led directly to the place where I was; and I knew and understood that they were coming, he to do my work at the bidding of her whose slave he was, while I and the sleeping girl were to be sacrificed to the black, cruel, revengeful lust of the Queen of the pigmy horde.

In a flash I was back in my normal state once more, looking at the crystal cube and its mysterious contents. I saw how the girl lay on a clear gleaming slab, wrapped in a robe similar to that which I was wearing, and which left one arm, exquisitely moulded, and half her breast exposed. Her face, perfect in the contour of its beauty, was calm and serene, as though she slept a peaceful, easy slumber, the dark lashes of her eyelids resting on her cheeks, and her lips lightly closed with a half-smile hovering round the corners.

At each angle of the slab there was a clear crystal bowl, in which was a deep crimson-purple liquid, on the surface of which a mass of luminosity, formed like a pyramid, floated and threw abroad a wonderful radiant light.

I was marvelling at the continuance of a flame in what seemed to be an hermetically sealed space, when, with a jarring, grating noise, one of the masses of quartz I had noticed on the wall at the other end of the chamber, swung back, and Tor Ymmothe, with the Hatter at her side, stood before me.

Back into my mind rushed the vision of a few moments ago ; back before my eyes came the spectacle of those shadowy forms with their mute, appealing looks, and I knew that the hour had come for some drama to be played, the significance of which I could not understand.

Over me there surged a great wave of hatred against the Yellow Queen and the man who stood beside her, and I grasped my revolver with a sinister and ugly motive in my heart. They saw me, and Tor Ymmothe uttered a shrill cry which echoed round the vault and rushed past me down the passages behind me, until I heard it echoing and echoing away in the distance of that cavernous tunnel and knew that it would soon return with terrible force and velocity.

"Quick ! Quick ! Speak the words," I heard her say to the Hatter.

I felt, rather than knew, what was in her mind, and, facing towards the sleeping girl, I shouted :

"Naggah ! Naggah ! Oom-moo-hah."

My voice rang through the cave and I

heard Tor Ymmothe moan as she fell forward on her knees, her glittering eyes fixed in a horrible stare upon the crystal cube.

The words echoed and shivered round the place and then whispered along the passages and through them just as the returning echo of Tor Ymmothe's cry came near. I remember how I stood calmly confident, as I knew the two volumes of sound approached one another, and waited for the result which the evil Yellow Queen feared so much. And, it came; came with a phenomenon that I shall never be able either to forget or to explain.

It was as though the words I had uttered met the returning volume of inarticulate sound, and absorbing the gathered strength of the latter, yielded to its impetus and rushed back to the chamber with the roar and speed of a mighty thunder-bolt.

They reverberated round the crystal cube and I saw the four flames quiver and leap. Then the sides of the cube split into a myriad of atoms; I saw the girl open her eyes, glance in wonder around her, and, with a cry in which joy and fear were strangely blended, spring to my side and cling to me just as, with a hissing sigh, the flames expired and left us in darkness.

Only one thing was visible; the phosphorescent form of Tor Ymmothe.

"Save me, save me from her," I heard in my ear.

"Dick, for God's sake, save me," came to me in the Hatter's voice.

The hatred and rage of a moment ago returned to me, but now it was against Tor Ymmothe alone; and, raising my revolver, I aimed at her gleaming breast and fired.

The noise of the shot sped away into the inner darkness as the unearthly form of the Yellow Woman fell heavily to the ground and lay, with dull lambent flames flickering and gleaming over it like the light on the sides of a fish when it hangs in the night.

The girl, grasping my arm tightly, cried in the Pitchorie tongue;

"Quick! Let us fly before the men can come."

"Hatter," I shouted. "Where are you? Come with us."

"Anywhere, anywhere," I heard his voice answer in a hopeless, lifeless way.

"Take his hand," my companion said, as she led me hurriedly forward, holding one hand and leaving the other free to grasp the Hatter as we passed him. I presume that she led us through one of the openings behind the blocks of quartz, but it was impossible to know more than that we suddenly found ourselves on a narrow ledge with a parapet in front of us and the roof low over our heads, just as the magnified report of my revolver shot crashed through the cavern, making the very rock tremble in the terrific vibration of the noise and clamour.

"We dare not go farther till they come," our guide whispered to us.

"Who are to come?" I asked.

"Why, those who threatened us just now, before Eilatow led us through the sacred temple into the place of the awful voices," she answered.

The Hatter gripped my arm.

"Silence, for God's sake, silence, till we get out; else I shall go mad," he whispered hoarsely.

I turned my head towards him as I heard his voice, and in so doing I caught sight of the phosphorescent gleam from the prostrate form of Tor Ymmothe on the right below us. It presented a horrifying sight in the dark and I felt the Hatter shudder and crouch down behind the parapet.

The next moment a racking din of yells and shrieks filled the air, and a ruddy light streamed through the masses of quartz on the wall of the cavern. Then they were pushed in and a crowd of the most hideously revolting looking creatures I have ever imagined, rushed through the openings, waving blazing torches over their heads, and howling and shrieking in an abandon of reckless defiance.

They were creatures who seemed to have been made up of an odd collection of limbs, trunks, and heads, and were in every degree of crippled malformity; one had a huge skull balanced on a body scarcely any larger than that of one of the pigmies; while another, with disproportionate limbs, had only a monkey skull upon its shoulders; another had tremendous arms on a lilliputian trunk, and another legs which were five times as large as they should have been. They were a nightmare, a vile nauseating spectacle, such as might come in the dark, lonely hours of night to mock and torment the stricken fancy of a diseased brain.

They rushed hither and thither as soon as they entered, until one of them noticed the prostrate form of the Yellow Queen. He howled in abject terror, and, flinging himself on the ground, crawled towards the body with fawning, snaky writhings.

The others stopped their pandemonium at his cry and grouped themselves behind him, advancing as he advanced, while through the doors behind them other forms crowded and pressed.

"Great heavens, he is growing," the Hatter gasped, and, as I looked, I saw that the grotesque form of the cringing creature was developing before my eyes into that of a powerfully built athletic giant.

From him I glanced at the others. They were all growing, and I turned sick at the spectacle and the horrible significance of it. Tor Ymmothe in her life had absorbed the vitality from her people until they had shrunk and shrivelled into the ape-like pigmies we had seen; but now that she was dead, the stolen forces of their bodies were returning to the forms whence they had been drawn by the diabolical arts of the Lemurian Queen.

The man crept along until he was near enough to touch the corpse of his slaughtered sovereign. As he neared her, I heard the returning echo of their cries coming nearer and nearer until, as he reached out his hand and touched her, the sound burst forth in a fury of uproar through the two passages.

The effect upon the horde of misshapen beings was indescribable. They faced round towards the sound and us, for as I now saw, we were in one of the passages but high up on a ledge near the roof. They evidently regarded the noise as a challenge, for with a renewed outburst of yells, they charged forward and through the passage.

I leaned over the parapet to watch them. The black pool was lit up by the glare of their torches, and across it the noise of their own cries was speeding. The foremost were at the water's edge before they realised what it was and then it was too late to stop, for the crowds were pressing fast upon their heels. They staggered and fell over the edge into the water and others followed so fast that soon the light of the torches of those who were behind lit up a scene of frightful and awful struggles.

The men, hideous in their half-completed growth, fought like demons one with the other, shouting and shrieking in every tone of frenzied rage and fear. And still fresh hordes pressed forward through the passages and surged across the floor of the cave, trampling the body of their fallen Queen out of all semblance.

"Come. Let us free the floods and measure justice to them all," the girl said quietly, taking my hand again, and drawing me forward ; while I, in turn, seized the Hatter's arm and led him unresistingly after me.

We walked along an upward sloping floor,

constantly turning from one side to the other until suddenly we saw in front of us the glare of daylight. A few seconds later we were standing on the summit of the wall which formed the rim of the upper reservoir. Our companion ran forward to a long level stone and sprang upon one end of it with all her weight. It sank slowly at that end and rose at the other, and she scrambled back from off it as it swung into an upright position ; and we heard a great rush of water down below, mingled with the shrieks and shouts of the struggling hordes.

"It is done. Now, let us seek Eilatow and tell him how we have done the task he set us," she said, turning to us.

As she turned, her glance wandered away over the stretch of desert which lay below us. She raised her hands to her head and screamed.

"Look! Look!" she cried. "Where is the city? Where are the temples and the palaces? Where are—oh, what is it?"

Her eyes met mine with an agony of fear in them.

"Speak! Tell me of this mystery," she cried.

"Do not fear," I said. "You are safe now. I will tell you presently."

I placed my arms around her, for I feared she

would fall and——well, there was something in my heart which bade me do it.

She looked at me steadily for a moment.

" The robe is that of the altar priest and the face is the face of my love. Why then should I heed, seeing that you and I are at last together ? " she said.

" Look at the lower pool," the Hatter exclaimed in English, bringing me back from a misty dreamland I was fast drifting into.

I glanced downwards. The water in the pool below us was agitated and boiling, and presently it rose over the rocky rim which circled around it and fell with a roaring thunder over the sides, while that in the pool beside us whirled round and round in a seething foam.

" The gates have broken," the girl cried. " The city will be swept away."

She threw her arms in the air and fell back in a swoon against me.

" Help me with her," I exclaimed, as I laid her gently on the ground.

The Hatter did not answer ; and, glancing up at him, I saw him standing, looking down at her with an expression of the most hopeless sorrow on his face that I have ever seen.

CHAPTER XXI.

TO DUST AND ASHES.

VIEWED from a latter point of view in the course of events, I feel that my action was cruel and selfish; but at the moment I was irritated beyond measure at the attitude the Hatter had assumed.

Had he resisted the influence of the Yellow Queen when we were together in that chamber, and had agreed to stand by one another, all the later trials I had undergone would have been avoided. I did not stop then to consider that, had it not been for those trials, I should never have discovered the girl, for whose welfare I was so much concerned. I could only revile the Hatter for his indifference in not coming at once to her help and my own.

But my words fell upon deaf ears, for he did not even raise his eyes, only did he stand staring down at her and murmuring under his breath, "How like! how like!"

In my impatience I lifted up the girl's form

in my arms, and carried it towards a spot where a boulder of loose rock threw a slight shade. There I laid her, taking off my gorgeous robe and rolling it into a pillow for her head.

"It will terrify her when she comes to," I heard the Hatter say at my elbow.

"What will?" I exclaimed angrily, as I turned towards him.

"To see you in those clothes. Don't you understand? She does not know that she has lain through unnumbered centuries of time, while the whole world has been changing. She thinks you are her lover."

"And so I am," I answered fiercely.

A spasm of pain passed over his features and contracted them, and he put up his hands to his eyes for a moment.

"Dick, my boy, you will know when you get back. We won't quarrel now," he said sadly, extending his hand to me.

I would have taken it; but my charge sighed at that moment, and I could only attend to her.

"She is coming to," I said softly, and he came and bent over her.

She opened her eyes slowly and let her glance dwell on my face. There could be no mistaking the love which shone in their deep, brown, liquid depths ; and, as I saw it, I felt my heart leap and tremble as I never had known it to do before. Then her glance wandered from my face to my costume and she started up.

" Who and what are you ? " she cried in a terrified tone of voice.

" I am he who found you just now," I said soothingly. " See, my robe is your pillow."

She glanced round at it.

" But these ? Whence came you that you wear such clothes ? Your face is——". She broke off with a scream. " Oh, tell me what it is ? Tell me, tell me," she cried excitedly. " What has occurred since we met ? "

" You remember all that took place, then ? " asked.

" Yes, of course. I was to have been handed over to the priests of the altar to be sacrificed, because I would wed none but you, my beloved ; and my blood was to keep the altar wet after they had laid you on it and offered you up in sacrifice. But Eilatow promised to substitute the priest, whom he hated, for you, and was to enable us to escape. And I waited for you to come ; waited ; waited ; until in weariness I slept and you came just now to rouse me."

I looked over at the Hatter who was sitting

on the ground on the other side of her, for I felt that I could not tell her anything.

He interpreted the appeal of my look and rose to his feet.

"Do you remember me?" he asked.

"Why yes, you are the stranger who brought the rebuke to the king and who——they said they had killed you," she broke off. "How did you escape? Not many can elude the vengeful vigilance of the priests of the crimson altar."

"I did not escape," he said solemnly.

"But you are here," she answered. "How could you be here, if you had been killed?"

"It is a terrible story," he went on. "A terrible story and I, in the learning of it, nearly lost my reason. How then shall I tell you?"

She looked at me.

"You are the one I love and the one who faced death for my sake?" she asked simply.

"Yes, and would face it again," I exclaimed passionately, as I took her hand in mine.

"Then what does it matter?" she said, as her fingers closed round mine. "We are together, and what does it matter, even if all the world were dead and gone from memory while love remains?"

"All the world you knew has gone from memory," the Hatter said gravely.

She glanced away across the desert and round upon the desolate rocks that rose on every side, and then her eyes sought mine again and her hands clasped mine more tightly.

"I do not understand," she said slowly. "Only do I know that you, whom I love, are here. Let me sleep again. I am so weary."

Her eyelids drooped, and she lay back upon my folded robe, breathing slowly and faintly, while I watched her with a fearful growing dread in my heart.

I felt a hand on my shoulder and heard the Hatter's voice in my ear.

"The time has come for the soul to return to earth once more, and it is seeking for its new body. Have patience, my boy, your lot is easier than mine, for you will find her again while I have lost her for ever."

He sank down upon his knees and fell forward, with his head on his arms, his frame shaking with great spasms of grief.

Over me there stole a sense so awful and so mighty that I was powerless to move or speak. Only could I hold the hands of the woman I loved, and watch her bosom slowly rise and fall with her faint breathing ; and, as I watched, I knew, by some subtle intelligence which filled me with dread, that soon the breath would cease to come.

Presently her eyes opened once more. A sweet, soft smile came over her face, and into her eyes there crept a look of rapturous love that thrilled me into an agony of passion. Then it gradually faded away into a dreamy far-off vacancy, and from her lips there came the words :

" I am waiting ; waiting ; waiting ; with our new and grander race."

The Hatter rose at the sound of her words and came to my side.

" Come, my boy, come," he said gently. " The shock may be too much."

I turned my head round with fierce words upon my lips, and as I did so, I felt my fingers close upon themselves. A shuddering awe swept over me and I felt my blood run cold. I glanced down. My hands were clasping air, and where a moment before I had seen that lovely face, there was only a heap of dry grey dust sprinkled over the garish robe.

CHAPTER XXII.

THEORETICAL HISTORY AND TRAGIC REALITY.

THE shock was so sudden and the blow to my senses so horrible that, for a time, I sat mutely staring at the gleaming robe which lay on the ground, and which so lately had enveloped a lovely living form. It was difficult to realise at the moment the full significance of the awful event, and I was as one in the dark, groping my way in search of some tangible reality which I could grasp, and assure myself that I was actually in a material world and not in one peopled with vapid shadows, which gathered and dispersed in the twinkling of an eye. Had it not been for the robe before me, I should have doubted my senses to the extent of attributing the whole occurrence to a mere passing delusion. But there was the robe before me, real and substantial, and within it the ashen dust was visible when I lifted up one corner.

It was too tangible a thing to be ignored, and so I was prevented from regarding all my experience as a dream, a dream of sweet and entrancing beauty mingled with grim horror and despair. It was only too real.

My memory, saturated with the influence which that beautiful being had shed upon me, retained her image in all its glorious detail. Her wonderfully soft and expressive eyes ; her full, rich, ruddy lips ; her rounded cheeks and her wealth of dark hair ; all were as clear to my mental vision as they had been to my physical sight only a few moments before. But that was all I had, and ever should have, I thought in my agony of mind, to treasure and remember.

As the thought came to me of the utter eradication of her whom I loved, I leaped to my feet in a fury of madness. She who had been in earthly life but just now, had gone across the boundary into that other world in which we all believe and yet cannot reach save· through the portals of death. She could not have gone very far, I thought. I would go after her, and I sprang forward to leap over the cliff which was within a few feet of me.

I felt myself thrown to the ground, and as I fell forward, strong arms clasped me.

It came to me that it was of no use to argue with him. I would let him have his way now, and when night came I would go and join her whom I loved.

"Thousands of years ago," he continued, " you loved the woman you saw to-day. The completion of your love was denied you, for you were slain, the body of you, that part which manifested the love in your senses. But you, the real being, could not be slain. The race of which you were a unit had acquired many a power which we have not yet been able, in this later growth, to realise. It was those powers which wrought the doom of that race in the universal working of the great law of compensation, as it will in the distant future work out ours also, should we abuse the knowledge in the same way. But for a time that bygone people held and controlled those powers, and used them, in the folly and vainglory of their arrogance, to wreak upon you and her a greater vengeance than the mere slaying of your bodies. Yours was slain ; but hers was so placed that as the æons of time rolled on, her soul would remain chained to her material form, both being devoid of sense, and incapable of change. You sought for her, the twin star of your being, in all the realms of life, but could not find her, for she was here, bound and imprisoned, and only to be set free when you, in the body, came back to her, and burst the bonds that held her. Then her soul, freed from the thraldom of inertia, sped through the space of eternity, through the vastness of time, through the immeasurable vastness of creative epochs, to the body which had grown for her occupation. And there you will meet her and recognise her, and complete the sequence of natural existence which the diabolic powers of perverted humanity strove to destroy thousands of years ago."

As his words fell upon my ears, a wave of conflicting emotions passed over me. Improbable as his theory sounded to me in my everyday, matter-of-fact habit of thought, it yet seemed to me to contain a greater amount of truth than I could rationally justify. The recollection of that vision which had come to me, when I was on the steamer on my way out to Australia, returned to my mind. There was the insatiable longing which had preceded it, a longing to leave all that which was ordinarily attractive and enjoyable, to return to the rough-and-ready life of the Australian bush ; to leave the pleasure and fascination of civilised life in the foremost city of the world, to come back to the barren wretchedness of an inhospitable, sandy desert. By what practical, modern, material view could that be justified or explained, I asked myself? But how intelligible it became, if one could accept the idea of previous existence with a connecting chain of influences, reaching from one life to the other.

More than that, the idea was balm to my stricken spirit. The love that had come to me so suddenly, and with such overwhelming strength, leaped and thrilled me as I clutched at the shadowy hope of once more meeting with the object of it. If she really lived, this girl, for whom I knew no name, save the gentlest, sweetest word I understood, what would I not do to meet her again?

"Tell me how I may know that it is true," I exclaimed, in my new-found fervour.

"Your own perceptions tell you already," the Hatter answered. "Believe in them—and remember that it is a very long time since we tasted food."

He commenced eating with the haste of a man who has the ravenous hunger of starvation upon him, and as I watched him I felt my mind grow calmer.

"If I could only know," I said.

"My boy, don't make one mistake," he exclaimed. "All the mystical side of life we may not know, but we do know the practical. Don't make the mistake that many do, of losing sight of the practical in a mist of speculations about the mystical. We cannot live without food. Eat while you may."

He resumed his meal, and after one or two ineffectual attempts on my part to bring him back to the train of thought he had been in before, I followed his example, and by the time that the sun sank out of sight, I had at least acknowledged the needs of a practical life, even in the midst of more than a mist of speculation about the mystical.

As we lay back on our blankets after our rough, but welcome meal, we lit our pipes and lay smoking in the calm, warm air of the tropical night. It would not have required an inordinately imaginative mind to have regarded everything which had occurred since we last lounged so and smoked as a phantasy of the brain. But there again the presence of one of those ancient robes belied the imagination, a robe which, if the Hatter's theory were correct, had served to grace religious ceremonials thousands of years ago, and now served to demonstrate to two rough-and-ready bushmen, that their senses were not belying them.

It was a curious contrast from then to now, and I broke the silence to ask the Hatter what form of religion had been served by the priests whose robes we had worn.

"A religion of brutalised humanity," he answered. "What we know now as science had been developed to a degree of perfection, far beyond anything we have as yet reached. But, unhappily for the race, the prevailing religion of the day was not forced from its position of ignorant arrogance by the discoveries of investigators. Instead, the powerful priesthood dominated the investigators, and retained for their own use the benefits which should have been spread over the whole world, with the result that, as the knowledge of man increased, the bulk of humanity sank lower and lower, weighed down by the greed and avarice of the unscrupulous combination of miracle-mongers. It is not difficult to understand what took place. Suppose for a moment that in these modern times, all the great discoveries and inventions were retained and controlled by a corrupt priestcraft. Just imagine the effect upon a superstitious race in our own time that a conscienceless body of men could produce, if they had an intimate knowledge of electrical appliances and the people none. How many miracles could be wrought by the telephone alone? And so it was with the people of Lemuria, and our great advance upon them, and our enormous development is due, not alone to the discoveries we have made, but to the fact that those discoveries are the property of the people and not of the priests."

"But what did they worship?" I asked.

"The people worshipped the priests, and the priests worshipped themselves, as they always do, sooner or later, when they have entire control. You can prove that to-day in those out-of-the-way places, where the medicine man, the witch doctor, and all the other local religious potentates, whatever their names may be, are invested with a supernatural halo."

"How do you know all that?" I asked.

"I learned it while I was in there," he answered. "Some of it I had thought out for myself before; I don't know how nor why; but when I heard her speak of it there was nothing strange in it to me."

"You mean Tor Ymmothe?" I said.

"Who else?" he replied briefly.

"When I left you," I began, "in the room

where the water was coming. What took place after that ? How did you escape ? "

" Easily enough," he said. " She opened another panel and I did as you did, sprang through it ; only she came through as well. You should have stayed with me then," he added sadly.

" Do you remember what you did ? " I asked. " How you went over to her and left me, and—— "

" Yes, I know," he answered dreamily. " That is what you do not understand yet, and I cannot tell you now. When you reach Wonga again you will know. The curse of my existence has ever been——you will learn it then," he broke off.

" But how are we to get back ? " I exclaimed.

" I never shall," he answered. " Even if I would, I could not. For you the way is open, and you will travel it, though I cannot tell you how."

I was more anxious to hear all that had transpired between him and the Yellow Queen and turned the conversation back again.

" But what took place after I left ? " I asked again.

" When I first went in with the other two, she obtained control over me," he said. " I fought against it, but I was powerless against it until I had you with me. All that really occurred after you had escaped I do not know. I only have a vague recollection of her speaking to me, and all she said at once became absolute truth to me. Then we went together up those stairs, and on the way she told me that I had to kill you, but I did not want to when I saw you."

"To kill me?" I exclaimed.

"Yes, it was either that I killed you, or that you killed her. She had tried to master you and failed, and when you fled she tried to overtake you, but somehow you eluded her, and then her only chance was to make me awaken the sleeper and slay you. But there again fate was against her, for you managed to reach the room where the girl lay, before we did; how I do not know, for she said that there was only an entrance on our side, and she was certain you would never find it. She told me all about the place we were going to."

He ceased speaking, and I exclaimed: "Go on, tell me the whole story."

"I thought I heard something," he said. "However, I will finish first."

His voice was strangely monotonous, and the horrible thought I had had before recurred to me. Was he really sane, or was he still under the influence which bade him kill me? He resumed his story as the idea came to me, and I grasped my revolver to be ready should my fears be well founded. As he spoke, he rose and took off the robe he was wearing.

"The range over there is an old volcanic outlet," he went on, in the same dreary monotone. "It was extinct when Lemuria was in existence, and the priests explored the crater and the cavernous tunnels which ran off from it. Some they built up into chambers, such as those we were in, chambers connected by a labyrinth of passages. The two craters above they filled with water, which they used as a vast source of hydraulic power, and to illuminate the subaqueous structures, they used their chemical knowledge to produce what the old alchemist brotherhood claimed to have known, but at which modern science scoffs, and that is, the oil of gold, a liquid which has the property of burning almost eternally so long as it is in vacuum, giving off a power of illumination that loses nothing either by reflection or refraction. It was in the vacuum chamber where the lamps were kept that they placed the girl whom you would have wed, after sending her into a deep cataleptic trance, which was to endure until air reached her, and she heard the words you somehow learned and used, a contingency they held to be beyond the bounds of possibility. The only chance of her being able to snap the first link in the chain that bound her was in the revival of volcanic activity, but that they did not anticipate for ages upon ages. Behind the chamber where she lay, there was a curious combination of passages and caverns which had the extraordinary power of magnifying sounds by some inherent acoustic properties, and this the priests made use of as a means of terrifying the people, for they so constructed the passages and the chambers between this cliff and the echoing gallery, that a word spoken in front of the gallery roared through the opening in the cliff with the voice of thunder."

" But I found that——" I began.

" You found the gallery and shouted for help, and it was the echo of your cry which came to us and made us hasten to the sleeper so as to defeat you and waken her before you reached her. Then we should have destroyed not only her but you also."

As he stopped a dull rumble sounded through the air.

" Is that thunder ? " I exclaimed.

A horribly discordant laugh came from my companion.

"Thunder!" he yelled. "Yes, the thunder of your doom. You who slew her and robbed me of my life; you whom I have saved up till now, so that I might see you perish in the flames of the fires you have let loose. You——"

A frightful crash stopped his words and a glare of lurid light lit up the scene. I glanced towards the range and saw the red flames leap up in the sky, and then I faced the Hatter.

He was standing with his face turned towards the glare and with his arms outstretched, and another fiendish laugh came from his lips as he shouted,—

"Blaze! blaze! Let the fires of hell come forth to burn the curse away."

I crouched down as he raved and shouted the most terrible anathemas at the blazing mountain. Then he sprang towards me, shouting,—

"Come! We will run and meet it!"

I sprawled over in my attempt to spring on one side and he, grabbing at me, just missed me. He tried to turn but could not stop, and with a cry of dismay I saw him fall headlong from the tree.

I looked down and saw him scramble to his

feet and run blindly to and fro, yelling and laughing that terrible laugh. The light gleamed on the robe he had been wearing, and I snatched it up and hurled it from me. It fell down to the ground, and as the Hatter saw it he leaped towards it and jumped upon it in an abandon of fury.

Then a terrific crash sounded and in an almost blinding glare I saw the rock split in two. For an instant the water, gleaming with the blaze above it, stood still, ere with a roar it fell forward, foaming and rushing. In a moment it had passed over the space between me and the cliff, and was surging round me and over me ; and with the noise of a hundred thunder-peals roaring in my ears, I felt myself borne resistlessly onwards.

CHAPTER XXIII.

ACROSS THE DESERT.

My next recollection was to find myself, bruised, sore, and exhausted, lying on the sand of the desert.

I raised myself on to my elbow and looked around me. My clothes clung to me, wet and cold, and the sand below me was wet also, while away in the distance I could see the ugly red glare of the volcano, and the noise of loud explosions came to me.

Then fear, wild unreasoning fear, took possession of me, and, starting to my feet, I ran forward without any thought save that of escaping. I ran till my breath grew short and my limbs ached and trembled, but still I plunged forward; now sinking up to my ankles in the soft wet sand, now stumbling in my stride and staggering down on to my hands and knees. There was a panic in my brain and it lent me a strength that would not recognise either exhaustion or fatigue. Through the whole

"I ran till my breath grew short, and my limbs ached and trembled." [*Page* 280.

night I staggered and stumbled forward, with only one idea of direction, and that away from the place where the red lurid glow in the sky told me the range was situated. I must have covered a very considerable distance in my terrified run, for when the sun rose above the horizon and I looked back, I could only see a cloud of smoke hanging above the sky line where I expected to see the loom of the range. I could not believe that I had run out of sight of it; rather did it seem to me that the whole mysterious structure had been swallowed up in the convulsion.

Now that the sun was up, I began to feel the effects of my flight. The efforts I had been putting forth for hours past had left me weak and thirsting, and now that the impetus of fear had passed away with the appearance of the sun, I was cognisant that my throat was parched and my limbs and body weary. My head was bare to the fierce heat of the sun rays, which grew in intensity at every moment, and my heart failed me when I recalled all that had recently occurred, and remembered the hopeless condition I was in to attempt the journey across the sterile wastes before me. I had neither food nor water with me, let alone a horse, to help me over the stretch of desert which lay between me and watered country. And worse than all, I was in ignorance of the direction I should take to bring me to the nearest point where I could obtain shade from the sun and water to revive me. I had turned towards the sun when I first saw it rise above the horizon, without heeding in what direction my face was before I turned; and now I did not know whether I was retracing the course I had followed during the night or not. I tried to rally myself by regarding the cloud on the horizon as being above the site of the range, and, turning my back upon it, I trudged forwards, tearing part of my shirt away so as to form some covering for my head.

Soon my tongue began to dry and my throat grew more and more parched, until it was almost cracking, while my eyes ached with the glare of the sun on the sand, and my spirits drooped as I looked despairingly ahead and saw only the same interminable stretch of glaring yellow waste. My one idea was to keep going forward, and I kept my feet moving till my senses left me and I reeled and fell.

I remember, every now and again, coming to myself and finding that I was lying with my face to the sand, digging my fingers into it in the hopes of being able to reach down to a cooler spot than the surface. Then I would stagger up and forward again, until my strength gave out and I fell once more. I lost all count of time ; I forgot what I was doing ; only the agony of thirst remained constant with me until I fell and failed to rise again.

I learned afterwards that a party of blacks, skirting the desert, had seen the glare of the volcanic fire, had pressed forward in order to ascertain what it was, when they descried me staggering along. They came up to me soon after I had fallen for the last time, and, seeing how matters were with me, had carried me back to the camp they had left in the morning, where there was a small water-hole. There they tended me, I know not for how long, for when I did get water it was only just in time, and brought back the flicker of life within me, to set me face to face in a struggle with a raging fever.

All that I remember of that period is a haunting vision of a beautiful figure, which constantly danced before my eyes urging me to go forward, while a hideous ogre clung to my neck and held me to the ground. So persistent was the vision that, even when I recovered my wits and found myself stretched out, thin and weak, under the shelter of a native gunyah, I saw the form dancing and smiling at me and beckoning me to come to it, among the few stunted trees that grew round the water-hole.

But I was too emaciated to attempt to follow it, and for weeks I must have hovered between life and death, with my mind more often wandering than not. The blacks used to share their food with me, and in the intervals, when my mind was fairly clear, I tried to make them understand that I wanted to get to the coast. Perhaps they understood, but I do not suppose I shall ever know; for one day as I was sitting listlessly in the shade of the gunyah, trying to piece some intelligible scheme out of the jumble that was in my mind, I heard an English tongue.

I sprang to my feet and glanced around me. The camp was deserted of blacks, but two white men on horseback were approaching the waterhole. I cried out in the wildness of my joy, and fell senseless to the ground.

The story that they told me when I came to myself again was full of interest to me. They were two of a party of seven prospectors, who had pushed forward in the hopes of being able to discover the whereabouts of a veritable El Dorado, which had been reported to be in the vicinity of the desert. About a month before, they said, a horseman had arrived at a mining camp some hundreds of miles beyond Coolgardie and had applied to the local police constable for an escort. The matter had been kept a secret until the arrival from the head-quarters of a sub-inspector and twenty constables, and the men of the camp then heard that the horseman was one of two mates, who had struck it rich away out back and had brought in a camel team loaded with great nuggets of gold.

The escort had started before the news leaked out, or else the chances of the two men retaining all their gold would have been very small, for the patch that the camp was working was terribly poor and the miners were nearly all cleared out of cash. A general stampede ensued as soon as the real destination of the troopers was known ; but when they found the team, it was guarded by the police, and not even the desperately hard-up miners cared to try conclusions.

But one of the two men gave them the whereabouts of the find, and by the next morning everybody in the township had cleared to track it out. Seven of them had started out together, and had stuck together ever since, but no sign had they been able to find of the range the two men had spoken of

"But what are you doing?" one of them asked me.

"I was prospecting with a mate, and we struck the desert and got done for water. I don't know what became of my mate, but the blacks found me almost dead and brought me here, and here I've been ever since," I answered.

I guessed who the two men with the camel team were, but I did not tell my rescuers all I knew about them. A mention of the range would only have led to a continuance of the journey in search of what I believed had long since disappeared. And now that I heard that Bill and Oates had reached settled country again, I only had one desire, and that was to do so too, and start away for England.

They took me back to the spot where the remainder of their party were camped, and I pitched them so horrible a tale of my own experience in the desert that they decided to regard the tale of the fabulous range as a traveller's story put up to deceive them, and return back to Coolgardie again. We started the next day, my new mates setting me on a spare horse they had; and I never was so pleased as when I really had my back turned on that desert which had been the scene of such terrible events in my life.

But if my new-found friends brought me luck, I did the same for them ; for a week later, when we were nearing the settlement, I chanced upon a find which has since developed into one of the biggest things in the Westralian field.

We were making our camp for the night, when I wandered off into a patch of scrub to try for a shot at some wallabies I had seen making for it. I chanced upon one just as it was leaning forward browsing, and fired at it, bowling it over. I ran over to pick it up and, as I approached it, I saw where my bullet had struck the ground before hitting the wallaby and had ploughed up a small furrow. Out of idle curiosity I ran my finger along the furrow, to find what had turned the bullet upwards again ; and, in doing so, saw something gleam in the soil. I stooped to examine what it was, and found a splinter of gold. A few moments later and I had torn back the shallow turf, and exposed a blobby excrescence of almost solid metal.

My shouts brought my comrades to the spot, and all ideas of a camp were forgotten in the joy and excitement of the discovery. A huge fire was lit, and, by its light, the soil was thrown back sufficiently to expose enough gold to make every one of us a rich man. Subsequent development showed that the gold was only on the surface, just a " blow," as they term it, of metal in a cup-like hollow ; but there was enough to satisfy us, and whatever the ultimate shareholders may think of it, we had no reason to grumble at the " Lucky Shot," as we named the claim.

For my own part, I was not particularly anxious to share in the find, because I knew that my share in the wealth Bill and Oates had taken away would be more than ever I could spend ; but my mates insisted that I must stand in with them ; especially as I was the discoverer. So we decided that two of us should ride on to the nearest township for a supply of stores and, while one returned with the stores, I would ride on to the coast, leaving it with the others to forward my share of the gold to my London bank.

As soon as I could I made my way back to Albany, and from there rode out to Wonga. My curiosity to read the manuscript, which I knew contained the history of the Hatter's life, was very keen. I had often wondered whether he too had escaped when the waters of the reservoir burst down upon us. It seemed very improbable to me that he should have done so, for the flood must have reached him where he stood on the ground, even before it reached me in the branches of the tree; and while I was borne along on the top of the rush, he must have been overwhelmed and drowned. There was no doubt in my mind as to the mental condition he was in at the time, and I doubt whether he would have made an effort to escape, even had it been possible.

Such thoughts recurred to me, as I rode slowly along the track which led to the humpy on Wonga; and I was doubtful whether or not to expect to find him at the place.

At Albany I had heard about the departure for London of two men, who had carried away with them, not only very heavy bank drafts, but almost an incredible amount of gold in bullion. The men, it was rumoured, had chanced upon the gold in that locality which is usually located in Australia as "out back," but they were very reserved about it otherwise, and kept both their knowledge and their company very much to themselves up to the time of their departure.

I again concluded that the two were Bill and Oates, and wondered whether they had visited Wonga before leaving, or whether they had given both the Hatter and myself up for lost.

19

CHAPTER XXIV.

THE HATTER NAMED.

THERE was no sign of human occupation about the humpy when I passed through the slip-rails on to Wonga. The door was closed; no smoke came from the chimney, and grass, sheltered from the sun by the verandah, grew rank and strong, where it would soon have been trodden down by any one coming and going through the doorway.

I rode up to the deserted-looking place; and, taking the saddle and bridle from my horse, turned it into the small fenced paddock beside the hut. Then I went round to the window at the back; and, opening it by the trick the Hatter had showed me, I scrambled through it into the one room of the interior. As I crossed the floor to open the door my eye caught sight of some white chalk marks scrawled on the wall, and I read, " B. and O. clearing. D.H. or H. write Saxted."

Both Bill and Oates had been out, then I

thought, as I read the vague message; they evidently believed that the Hatter and I were still likely to turn up, though how they could think so, when they had taken all the horses and camels with them when they started, I did not know. The latter part of the message showed that they had gone home; and I was satisfied that all the references to the two rich but uncommunicative miners that I had heard, related to my quandom mates.

I opened the door, and brought in my saddle and swag; and soon I had a fire blazing up the chimney and a billy of tea on to boil. While it was brewing I drew the line from the two posts and located the spot where the Hatter had constructed his secret hiding place. It was an easy task, and I had the packet of manuscript out, as well as the money I had placed there, by the time my tea was ready. I had my meal with the packet lying in front of me on the table, the while I speculated as to its contents; and when I had finished I lit my pipe and opened the waterproof wrapper.

Inside I found a second wrapper of paper, on which was written: "To my friend and comrade, Dick Halwood. If this falls into other hands than his, will the finder gratify the wishes of a dead man and destroy it, unread."

An eerie feeling crept over me as I read this inscription. The manuscript had fallen into the hands he had intended it for, and I was entitled to open it, in accordance with his expressed wish ; but the latter part of the inscription struck me in an uncanny way. He, poor unfortunate, had little thought when he wrote it that I should take it from the place where he had placed it, with an uncertainty in my mind as to whether he was really dead or alive, but with the knowledge that he had more than once tried to do that which, had he been successful, would have prevented me from ever returning to the place where he had asked me to seek for it.

" Poor demented creature," I thought aloud. " He was not in his right senses then, for no truer, more faithful, comrade ever existed than he had proved himself to be ; and whatever he may have done, which was seemingly either treacherous or dishonourable, was not done by him, but by some hideous power which controlled him against his own better will."

I raised my eyes from the packet as I involuntarily spoke, and then I sprang to my feet ; for there, in the clear light of day, between me and the fireplace, stood the Hatter, clothed as I had last seen him, and with the gentlest smile upon his face that one could imagine.

"Great God! How did you————"

My tongue failed me before I could complete my excited exclamation; for the form, which was so perfectly clear to my eyes at the moment I raised them, had vanished even as I spoke.

I stood gazing at the place where it had appeared, and past me and over me there swept a momentary chill, as though a breath of cool air had blown upon me; in my ears there sounded a soft rustling, and I caught the words, " Good-bye and bless you, comrade "; and I 'rushed from the hut, quivering and unnerved, and stood in the clear, warm sunshine.

I sat down on a log for a time, until I managed to get some control over myself; and then, re-entering the hut, I quickly gathered up my swag, and rolling it up with the money inside, I put the packet of manuscript in my pocket and went out to saddle my horse. That done, I returned to the hut, scattered the fire upon the floor, closed the door, and, mounting my horse, rode away; for I felt that to have stayed inside that humpy any longer would have driven me mad. As the track turned away out of sight from the hut I glanced back, and saw the smoke bursting through the roof.

I did not draw rein until a score of miles lay between me and Wonga, and then it was only to ease my horse a bit, for I was determined to push right on to Albany. Fortunately the night was beautifully moonlight after the sun went down, and I managed to reach the township in time to secure a room in one of the hotels, long after midnight though it was.

I retired to my room and, locking the door, sat down to read the manuscript, the examination of which had been so strangely interrupted. Once I began it I could not stop until I came to the last word ; and I sat till the grey dawn came up, wondering and marvelling at the tale I had read—the life history of a strangely complex nature, to which only the final chapter was wanting ; and that I already knew. This is the story that I read :

"When you come to read this, you will understand what has hitherto confused you. As you bore with me in the past, bear with me now ; for I shall be what the world terms dead, although it is my steadfast belief that I shall be beside you at the moment, invisible to you, but conscious of your every thought and act. Therefore be merciful, for the hell of theology is the consciousness of the disembodied spirit to the full significance of its bygone bodily acts and thoughts, and the interpretation put upon them by those it loved on earth and loves still in the other world. Remember ! Of the dead speak only in kindness and think only in charity. The acts of men are decreed by the power of fate, and the ill deeds of one may be the salvation of many. Pity and forgive, but do not blame, until you know and understand what made me all I was, and then——think of me as I was to you, your mate and comrade, and not as the ruined, reckless scoundrel, Claud Digby, baronet and fool."

When I had read so far I raised my eyes, half-expecting to see before me again the vision I had seen in the hut. But there was only the commonplace detail of an Australian bush-hotel bedroom around me, and I was sorry it was so ; for in my heart there was a great yearning pity for my old comrade, and I would that I could have told him of it. Perhaps he knew, better than I could have explained to him, for he might after all have been right in his ideas, and he might have looked into my heart of hearts and seen and known my feelings and rejoiced. What human being could dispute it ?

With such thoughts within me, I turned the page over and read on. "I was born with the proverbial silver spoon in my mouth. The heir to an ancient title, insignificant in rank, perhaps, but second to none in ancestral glory ; with parents who doted on me and showered all that love could suggest upon me, and with a vast fortune as my future property, my childhood should have been one prolonged period of happiness and content. As I was well endowed in material things and physical appearances, so was I also fitted mentally to occupy a prominent position among my fellows. In every way except one ; and therein lies all the sorrow, the disgrace and the misery of my life, and of those with whom destiny allied me. Sometimes I have tried to reason with myself that it was the taint of insanity which was in my blood ; but it is a poor consolation, the poorer that it is not true. I was never mad. I was only dominated by some malevolent influence, created by my own folly in former periods of existence, for in the loneliness of my Australian life I have come near to those subtle forces which lie within all men's reach, and especially those who live in and with Nature ; and thus have I been enabled to look backwards upon the turgid currents engendered in bygone ages, and trace them from the single evil tendency, from which there has spread onwards a stream that has grown stronger and stronger in each successive swirl, until it has become the seething flood of murky influences which surge round me now.

"With a purer past I might also have learned to look forward; but the dense materialism of my being befogged my vision when I looked ahead, and only could I see trivial acts, and those the clearer by reason of their own stolidity. But the past I could see distinctly, and in it I recognised my evil genius, engendered until it took to itself sufficent strength and force to manifest itself as a separate entity and dominate my original nature, whenever that sought to assert itself and cleanse away the stains of its defilement. Being a man, the evil of my own creation took to itself the form of the opposite sex, and, as a woman, has overshadowed me and lured me downwards to the depths of my depravity.

"Strange that it should be so, and the more bitter, since in my life there has twice been given to me the means of escape from the thraldom of my sorrow; and both were the loves of women. The first was that of my mother; the second that of my wife. Either would have sufficed could I but have had them to understand, or could I but have seen clearly. But the mists of my own making obscured my vision, and they only realised, when it was too late, the power of the foe they had to meet.

" My mother understood it as she was passing away into the other world, and with her last breath implored me to seek and win the only means of strength, the love of a true-hearted woman. She looked down into my heart and saw the black, cold cruelty, the fiendish treachery and unscrupulous perfidy of my inner nature. Her mother's love for the one who owed his life to her did not quail at the sight ; rather did it look deeper and farther, until it recognised the underlying impulse, bound and weighted into inactivity, but with all its vitality un-impaired, if only it could be freed from its shackles and allowed to utilise its own potenti-ality. As it was, the influence of her words stirred my better nature, and for a time the other and the stronger side was held in sub-jection. Could I have met at that period the one whom I met later, the ultimate defeat of my evil tendencies might have been complete ; but it was not to be, and gradually the restrain-ing control wore off, until it only remained in a memory at which I scoffed and jeered as the remnant of a passing weakness, plunging the more into the slough of vice and iniquity. Only when I was steeped to satiety in wickedness did I meet the second angel in human form.

"At our first meeting I felt the demon at my elbow grow faint and weak, while the vestige that remained of my mother's influence revived; and in a fit of deep and abject remorse I foreswore my past course of life and sought, honestly and manfully sought, to effect my own reclamation. It was easy to win the love of that pure, sweet, innocent girl ; too easy, I have sometimes thought, for had the struggle been harder and longer I might have gained a greater ascendency over my unfortunate bent of iniquity. But not yet was my emancipation to be achieved ; for even as I felt myself surrounded by all those glorious and sustaining incentives, which come to a man who receives the love of a noble-hearted woman, my evil nature burst out into revolt—the more terrible that it had known something of restraint. The stream of destiny surged and bubbled round me, and I was swept away—a useless, thriftless derelict. In my mad fury I sought to pollute the purity of her whom I loved, and to drag her down from the pinnacle of her excellence, down to the degraded level that I occupied. She, barely realising the awful significance of it all, chided and counselled me with sweet, gentle kindness, which only maddened me the more ; and I deliberately planned and schemed to drag her, and all her family, down, by ruining them financially, since I did not seem to be able to do it morally.

"There, too, I failed; for the crash of material disaster only brought out the clearer and the stronger the noble attributes of their natures, and I fled from among my fellow-men, away into the nameless interior of Australia, where I wandered, a nameless, miserable wretch.

"Once I nursed the wish to rebuild the fortune I had squandered, not for my own use, but for the use of those I had wronged. For, strange and contradictory as it may seem, my constant desire was to benefit and succour them, even when I acted in such a way that I could only attain the reverse. In that lay the subtlety of my torture. Always was I conscious of what I was doing ; always was I awake to the terrible consequences of my acts; and always did I know and feel my own debasement ; even while I gloried in the treachery and the cruelty I was committing.

"For years I wandered in search of wealth, often with it just within my reach ; but the prospect was all that I ever realised, until eighteen years had gone by from the date when I fled from among my fellow-men. Then I

met you, and read in your face the character
I so sorely needed. Chance had thrown you
in my way; chance made you do what hundreds
of others had done—trust me, and believe in
me. And in that I knew lay my last opportunity
of beating back the demon I had created in
my past. Once more I resolved, and swore to
myself, never to betray or deceive you; and I
have kept my word. When we returned with
wealth enough for both, and enough for me
to buy back my lost estate, I put my ambition
from me; for once I robbed myself, and sacrificed myself, giving to you all that meant the
realisation of my dream of nearly twenty years.

"Nor was that the only sacrifice I made.
In the woman, the abnormal monster whom we
saw, I recognised the personification of the ogre
that had haunted me through all my life, and
with the chance of returning to my own land,
and strong enough at last to make some amends
for my evil past, I renounced it, and forced
myself to go back to where the, to me, hideous
and repulsive impersonation of my evil genius
dreed her miserable weird.

"But again I failed. All my efforts to reach
that place of horrible doom were frustrated,
until I cried in the agony of my helplessness,
even to make this poor amend for my wasted

life, for the help of the only human being who could aid me. For days and weeks I have been longing and striving to reach out to where you are, and tell you of my needs. As the time goes on, and you do not come, I turn to this idea and write down the story of my life, in the hope that, before I die, I may be able to send it to you, and that you may read it, and give me the one small thing I ask—your pity. Only a passing thought ; only one touch of human sympathy from one who now knows me as I am, and to whom alone, of all the world, I have been true and faithful. Then, wherever my soul may be ; however much it may ache in the sorrow and the misery I have prepared for it, a gleam of light will come ; and I shall know that one, at least, has not suffered from my acts ; that one, at least, has nothing to forgive in me ; that one, at least, remembers me without hate, but with the gentle kindness of regret."

CHAPTER XXV.

COVENTRY OF SAXTED.

As I sat on the verandah of the hotel the morning after reading the manuscript that the Hatter, or as I may now call him, Sir Claud, had left me, I was angry with myself; for, in spite of all that I could do, there was only one idea paramount in my mind, and that was to start for England directly a vessel came into the port.

All my life I had rather prided myself upon the sturdy practical view I took of things. When I had met men with curious opinions, as one sometimes does in that land of extraordinary contradictions, the great southern continent—it is folly to term it an island—I had always scoffed at them and twitted them that, for all their theories, it was to beef and mutton that they looked for the mainstay of existence; and beef and mutton it would be for all time.

Yet, a few months ago, I had deliberately
303

turned my back upon the material prosperity which was at my command in London—the very acme of my beef-and-mutton theory—to voyage out to Australia again. I had persuaded myself that it was the sunshine and the scent of the gums I was yearning for ; the romantic life of the swagsman tramping along the eucalypt-fringed roads, with his swag on his back and freedom in front of him. Well, I could see just such men from where I sat—men who were toiling along, perspiring and profane, what with the heat of the climate, and the dust of the road—and somehow the romance of the situation was not so evident now as it had been when I was comfortably settled in the capital of the world. But it was undoubtedly very strong within me then; or was it that I was weak in my practical view of things, and had allowed myself to be carried away against my better judgment?

It was useless trying to find the reason now. I had come from peace and comfort into restlessness and roughing ; and now, like a shifty weather vane, I was round on the other course with an overmastering desire to go back home again. There had been visions of a cosy little station in the balmy Australian atmosphere, where I could spend the rest of my days with a strapping Australian girl as my companion, and a crowd of young Australians growing up around me and giving me a reason for all I did. The realisation of that dream was possible now, but to my intense disgust I found that the attraction of it had passed. Instead of it I had another impulse, and that—to go home.

It seemed ignominious to give way to such a vacillating influence, and I struggled to persuade myself that the events of the last few months alone should be enough to keep me where I was. I tried to rouse my dormant enthusiasm for an Australian life, by recalling the scene upon that ridge, when the whole of my soul had gone out in a great love for the girl who had so strangely come into my life. Surely if she came back at all from the realm of mystery into which she had vanished, it would be in Australia that she would re-appear ; and therefore, on that ground alone, I should remain. So I reasoned with myself, but it was useless; I was beginning to discredit even my own memory.

The events which I recalled could not possibly have happened, I told myself. The fever that I had had before the prospectors found me with the blacks had caused me to be delirious, and the delirium had left these im-

20

pressions on my mind—and, to prove it was so, I would go home and seek out the men who had gone with us to that visionary place. It was not superfine reasoning, but it provided an excuse, some slight mollification of my out-raged pride of practical views of life; and I went and secured a passage to London by a steamer that was due on the morrow.

The sense of happiness and content which had come to me when I went on board the steamer in the Thames, on the day of my departure for Australia, came to me again when I embarked on board the "Ballaarat," in King George's Sound, and, steaming out of the harbour, I saw the coast line of Australia gradually fade out of sight.

The time occupied by the voyage passed on wings; and it seemed that scarcely a week had elapsed when once more I was on English soil, with a vague wonder in my mind as to how I had ever left it. Two days later and I was on my way to Suffolk, to seek out my quondam mate, at Saxted.

When I arrived at the station which the guide books told me was the nearest that the railway went to that sleepy, small, old-fashioned village, I found that I was still seven miles away from it. But as I arrived early in the afternoon the distance did not disconcert me. I engaged rooms in the village where the railway ended, and secured a conveyance to drive me out to Saxted Manor.

On my way thither I entered into conversation with the driver, in order to learn all I could about the family I was going to visit. Discounting the village gossip, with which the knowledge of my informant was very largely tinctured, I arrived at a result which was very much in accord with what I expected. Years before, the driver told me, the daughter of the house had been married to a " bad lot," as he expressed it, who had ruined all her family, and then deserted her and her child. The old place was sold; the father of the girl dying of a broken heart and the girl herself following soon after. Two sons remained, one of whom went to the wall, but the other—he was a perfect hero, according to his enthusiastic historian.

Geographical knowledge was somewhat of a hazy quantity in Suffolk, to judge by the succeeding remarks of my companion; for he averred that the last of the Coventrys of Saxted had voyaged to Australia, and personally attacked the country belonging to one of the native kings there; had been made prisoner

and doomed to lifelong slavery, but managed
to escape with all the king's treasure in a native
ship ; and had sailed about until he fell in with
a British man-o'-war, when he and his prize had
been towed into port, from whence he had
returned to the old village.   He had bought
back the family property from the man who
had secured it when the father had been sold
up, and was now electrifying the whole country
with his wealth, his magnificence, and the
wonderful tales of his marvellous adventures.
There was so much reverence in the man's
voice when he was speaking of the latest and
the greatest of the Coventrys, that I did not
like to tell him that the powerful magnate,
which provincial innocence had made him into,
had not so many months before been only
plain " Bill, the Axer," a hard working Australian bush-labourer, with no money to speak of,
and less prospects.   He would not have
believed me if I had ; so I left him with his
romance about the war with the native king
and the escape in the native ship, intact.
Romance in a Suffolk labourer is too rare and
brilliant a thing to be disturbed when it is met
with.

When we arrived at the old Manor I sent
him back to his village, and walked down the

approach to the house—a grand old red brick structure surrounded by ancient elms. I had not written to announce my coming; for at the time I left London I was not sure that Coventry had returned to the place, so that when I reached the door of the house and a servant answered my ring, I contented myself with sending in word that I wanted to see Mr. Coventry on business.

The servant left me standing where I was, and presently I heard the voice I had last heard in that far-off Australian desert the night we arrived at the oasis by the range. I turned away when his footsteps drew nearer, and only when I heard him asking my business did I face him. It was a thoughtless thing to do; for the shock when he saw and recognised my face was very great. He staggered back from the doorway.

"God!" he exclaimed. "Are you man or spirit?"

"Both," I answered. "Don't you know me—Dick Halwood?"

Away somewhere in the house behind him there was the sound of a girlish voice, and he grabbed my arm almost savagely.

"Come in here!" he exclaimed, as he pulled me across the hall and into a room which opened off it. "You scared the life out of me," he added, in an apologetic tone, when we were inside the room and he had closed the door. "Where did you come from, and where's the Hatter?"

"I reached London two days ago," I answered. "The Hatter is, I believe, dead."

He looked at me curiously, without speaking.

"And Oates?" I asked.

"Oh, he is all right; he is in Scotland now, I fancy. But you—we never expected to see you. We thought you were dead, and expected that the Hatter would come round some day and say so. It is all very strange, very strange," he went on.

There was a peculiar, distrustful air about him, and he eyed me in a suspicious way; his glance, when it met mine, giving me the impression that he was not overjoyed at my arrival. It occurred to me that he might be hungering after our shares of the gold, even if he had not already taken them for his own use.

"I suppose you remember me well enough?" I asked; not perhaps in the gentlest of tones, for the suspicion in my mind angered me.

"Oh yes," he answered shortly.

"I saw the message you left in the hut at Wonga," I continued.

"Oates left that. I did not go out, but stayed in Albany," he answered. "We realised all the stuff as soon as we reached this side, and, taking a fourth each, we banked the rest for you and the Hatter. You can have it whenever you want it."

His manner lost nothing of the restraint it had had during the first moment of our interview; and now that he had referred to the money, there was only one explanation of it in my mind. He did not wish to renew our acquaintance now that he had derived all the benefit he could out of it, and wished to give me the cold shoulder. The idea nettled me even more than his implied suspicion.

"Very good," I said shortly. "And what about the Hatter's?"

"I suppose it must wait till he comes," he answered.

"He has given me full power and instructions what to do with it," I said.

"Oh, has he?" he replied, as if my observation were of no possible interest to him, and my anger increased. If the man were going to treat me in this offhand manner, I was certainly not going to consider his feelings, as I had intended to do, in the breaking to him of the news as to who the Hatter really was.

"Of course you do not know what his real name was?" I asked.

"How should I? A man who says he is a hatter is nameless to any one who understands the rule of the bush. It is no business of mine to find out who or what he was."

"Excuse me, but it is," I rejoined curtly, still more irritated at his voice and manner. "The Hatter's real name was Sir Claud Digby."

I intended to surprise him, and I succeeded; for he turned ashen grey as I mentioned the name which, of all others, I knew he hated.

"What does it mean? What does it mean?" he exclaimed, staring at me vacantly.

"I have his written statement, which he left behind him at Wonga, in case he died while we were on that journey. If I am not mistaken, he was your brother-in-law, and the father of your niece," I went on maliciously.

The man stood staring at me after I had finished speaking, with an expression of vacant wonder on his face.

"He desired me to see that his child received his full share," I added.

"I don't understand it," he muttered. "It is too preposterous."

I took the words as being applied to myself, and I resented them immediately.

" Whether it is preposterous or not, it is a fact," I exclaimed warmly.

He looked up at me quickly.

" Forgive me, Halwood," he said. " I have been unintentionally rude ; but you do not know what all this means. I do not dispute your statement ; it is the coincidence that amazes me."

" It is my turn not to understand," I replied shortly ; for having been once nettled I could not smooth away my anger in a moment.

"I know," he answered quietly. " And as yet I cannot explain."

"I have no wish to pry into anything that does not concern me," I went on stiffly, and liking the man's manner less and less. " What I know is that which Sir Claud wished me to know and, also, to act upon. I am here now merely to carry out his wishes. He felt that he had injured all your family and, having made a fortune at last, he would have given it to you ; but as you, through his instrumentality, have made one also, his naturally goes to his child, of whose existence he was totally unaware. until you yourself told him."

" Yes, there it is again. There is more of the mystery. I met him, of all men in the world, and did not know him. Had I done so I should have most probably killed him ; but, instead of that, he enables me to make my fortune and I look upon him, my bitterest enemy, as my dearest friend. And now you come here ; you, who are even a greater conundrum.''

" My appearance need not inconvenience you," I retorted hotly. " Whatever conundrum there is——''

" My dear Halwood, this is no time for heroics," he said, interrupting me. " I should have preferred to have waited a little longer before accepting what appears to me to be a contradiction of everything that one usually regards as rational and tangible ; but you give me no option. Will you come with me ? "

He opened the door as he spoke, and walked along the passage outside, and I followed him. We crossed the fine spacious hall, hung round with old oil portraits, and then we ascended a wide stairway. At the top a passage ran at right angles to it and, turning to the left, Coventry stepped forward. I turned to follow. Then I leaped to his side and, gripping hold of his arm, held him, while I pointed excitedly to a picture at the end of the passage, which was so placed with regard to the light that the figure it contained seemed as though it were standing out from the frame.

But it was not that trick of the painter's art that startled me ; it was the face of the subject, a face wonderful in its beauty of feature and expression—and the face of the girl I had found lying in that far-off range in the sleep of death. So taken aback was I at the apparition that I could only stand grasping Coventry by the arm and pointing, but unable to utter a word. To my startled eyes the figure was smiling upon me as it advanced towards me.

"That is my sister's portrait; Lady Digby that was," Coventry said sadly. "It was painted before her marriage with—great Heavens, man, what is the matter?"

It was his turn to grasp my arm; for I should have fallen headlong to the ground as I heard his words. The shock of seeing the picture was bad enough, but the words I heard him utter recalled to me others that I had scarcely heeded at the time they were said.

Again I was standing on that distant ridge, bending over the fainting form of the girl I had found, and to my memory there came the Hatter's words, "How like!" and then the rest of the sentence, "I have lost her for ever, but you will find her again."

The emotion of love had lain dormant from the time that I had accepted the idea he had put forward that I was to live, to escape from the dangers of the desert, and come home again to find her. It had not died; only had it sunk peacefully down, waiting in patience till the time should come for it to manifest itself once more in the presence of its queen. Now that I stood before her portrait, recognising her, and knowing her in spite of the modern vestments she wore, as the later incarnation of my Lemurian bride, my love swept over me in a great wave of passionate impulse, and even in the midst of it came the cruel heartrending knowledge that too late by twenty years had I come to claim her.

The place seemed to spin round me; there was a dull roaring in my ears and my heart stood still. I dimly felt the grip Coventry had of my arm, and heard his voice speaking words I could not understand, and I knew that I was falling.

Something of his meaning penetrated the stupor that was upon me, and I made one effort to rouse myself. I saw him turn and hasten down the stairs, and my eyes went towards the picture again.

I raised myself up on my arms, staring in

wild terror, for there, between me and the picture I saw, more clearly than I could see the picture beyond, the form of the girl I loved. She was wearing the loose yellow robe she was wearing when I found her ; her face was towards me, and her eyes looked at me with an expression of such deep pathos and affection as to be almost reverence, while her arms were extended towards me, and her lips were parted in a soft, sweet smile.

A thousand fancies flashed through my brain, but only one was clear enough to be understood ; and that was the idea that I was on the point of death, and this was my disembodied love waiting to greet me beyond the pale. I essayed to spring towards her, but as I gained my feet I felt my head throb ; and, with the feeling that something had snapped in my brain, I fell forward into darkness and never-ending space.

CHAPTER XXVI.

THE UNKNOWN PORTRAIT.

MY next rational conception was to realise that I was lying in a remarkably cool and comfortable bed, in a room into which the scent of flowers came through the half-opened lattice window. That was all my eyes could see when I again consciously opened them, and I moved slightly in order to see more.

Immediately a nurse in a grey costume, with white cuffs and apron, appeared at my bedside ; and I blinked at her, the more puzzled that there lingered in my brain shreds of delirium night-mare, strangely blended with the familiar face and form of this girl. She smiled as her eyes met mine.

"Now you have had your sleep and I have chased them all away," she said. "They won't come back, I'm sure, but you had better take this and get strong in case they should."

She held out a cup to me, and I tried to put

318

out my hand for it ; but found that I could not raise my arm.

" I'll manage," she said, and, leaning over, she put the spout of an invalid cup between my lips, and slowly poured some liquid into my mouth. When it was finished she laughed softly and said, as she put the cup down :

" Now, if they do come, we will blow them all up quite easily."

" What do you mean ? " I asked, my voice so weak that I could scarcely hear it myself.

She turned quickly round and looked at me, placing her hand on my forehead at the same time.

" Oh, this is capital," she exclaimed. " But you must keep very quiet. You have been ill, and hurt yourself; but you will soon get well now. Just lie quiet and rest."

" But where am I ? " I asked, struggling to get some sense out of the muddle of my mind.

" In my care," the nurse replied brightly. " And if you are not pleased with that I shall be very much offended."

" But where, where ? " I queried, not to be put off. " This isn't Australia."

" Of course it isn't ; but if you are going off to Australia again I shall go away."

" Why ? " I asked.

Through the open window there came the sound of wheels on a soft gravel road.

" There's the doctor, and if you're not quiet now I don't know what will happen," the nurse said, as she smoothed my pillow ; and almost at the same moment, a man appeared at my bedside whose face was, like my nurse's, absurdly familiar to me and yet unknown.

He came and spoke to me softly, and then gave me something more to drink ; and I felt myself sinking into a peaceful sleep. When I next awoke, both the nurse and doctor were still there.

"I must have dozed for a second," I said, as I saw them.

" Yes, a few hours ago," the doctor answered, with a smile. " You will soon be all right now ; except the arm, of course."

" What arm ? " I asked.

" You don't remember. Well, I think you will be better if you know. You fell down the stairs, breaking your arm and damaging your head ; but we have got you over the brain part of the difficulty, and now you have only to pick up your strength and let your arm mend."

" And don't fight pigmies," the nurse added.

" No, don't fight any more pigmies," the

doctor echoed. "We don't want to have to set it again. Now I think you might see Coventry for a few minutes."

He turned away, and presently I saw Coventry approach my bedside.

"This is a great improvement," he said. "I'm glad to see you so much better, old man; don't worry, and we'll soon have you all right again."

"What does it all mean, Bill?" I said. "I don't understand."

"We'll tell you about it to-morrow, but you must go to sleep now," the nurse interrupted.

"They are in charge, old man," Coventry said; "but I'll come in again in the morning."

By the following morning I had advanced sufficiently along the road to recovery to be told something of my recent exploits. Coventry's version was, that I grabbed him by the arm and then fell, apparently in a swoon, to the floor of the passage on the top of the stairway. He turned to run down for some brandy, and had reached the foot of the stairs when I came crashing down after him, rolling over and over from the top to the bottom, smashing my arm and nearly fracturing my skull in the fall. After that I had naturally developed delirium, in which I only seemed to have one idea, and that was to slay the crowds of pigmies that surrounded me. But my efforts were not conducive to the knitting of my broken bones, and once the doctor had to reset my arm; after which I was carefully tied down, which explained my inability to move when I tried to.

"I knew what the pigmies meant, but they would only have laughed at me if I had said so, and I held my tongue," Coventry said.

"But the girl? What about the girl? She seems to have been here. I cannot quite remember. I saw her somewhere," I exclaimed.

"Oh, you mean the nurse. Yes, she has done no end for you," he said.

"No, I don't mean her. I mean—I mean *the* girl," I replied.

"Don't, old man. Get well; but don't worry over vestiges of your fever. You have mixed up the nurse with your dreams," he said quickly.

I wanted to dispute with him that it was not so; but he would not talk about it, and said that he would have to go away if I got excited. So I had perforce to keep my own opinion, for the nurse also declined to let me talk about the girl who haunted my mind. It was not until I was allowed to get up from my bed, that Coventry would talk about anything connected with our trip. But at last he was satisfied that I was well enough to hear his story, and then he told me.

He said that after being carried into the cave by the pigmies, he and Oates were kept together in a small, dark chamber, and allowed to hear and see nothing until the Hatter came to them and told them that they were to be set at liberty. His advice to them was that they should round up the team at once, load it with gold, and start without more delay than was absolutely necessary to try and find me. When they got outside again, they shouted and searched for me, and, as they could get no answer, they concluded that I had either been carried off as well, or killed. So they loaded up the camels, working with a will, which was not diminished by the fear of the horde once more pouncing upon them. By sunset they had everything ready and were away, not drawing rein until the range only showed as a shadow against the horizon.

The following days they pressed onwards until they struck timbered country, and from there they made their way into a settled district halting on the outskirts of a camp until they obtained a police escort. A few days later they were on board a steamer at Albany, with most of the gold, in bullion, in the strong room.

He detailed their experience in just as many words as I have used, and stopped short at the departure from Albany.

" But after you arrived here ; what did you do then ? " I asked.

" Oh, we were all right, then. But how did you manage to get clear ? " he inquired.

I hesitated a moment before replying. There was a manifest anxiety on his part to avoid, or at all events to postpone, for as long a time as possible, a full statement of his own doings after he had arrived in his own country again. I could only interpret this as being in some way connected with what I had told him about the Hatter. It seemed useless on my part to try and induce him to talk freely on the subject until I had given him the information he desired about myself. So I at once entered into an account of my experiences, from the moment when I had shouted to them from the top of the cliff to the time when I arrived at his house. He listened without once interrupting me, but with a keen and close attention.

" What an extraordinary story," he said, at length, when I had finished my recital. " If I had not seen the pigmies for myself, and penetrated a little way into their cavernous dwelling, I should not hesitate to regard it as a piece of wild imaginings of utterly impossible events. But I cannot, in the face of my experiences."

"There is yet a stranger part to tell," I said.

"Why, I thought you said you had told me all from the moment that you shouted to us, until this?" he exclaimed.

"No, I said to the moment when I arrived at your house," I answered. "The strangest part comes afterwards, at least to my way of thinking."

He look at me with questioning eyes.

"Finish your story," he said quietly.

"When you were showing me up the stairs," I said, "I saw a portrait hanging at the end of the passage."

"Quite right," he answered. "It was the portrait of my sister."

"It is the portrait or the girl I found in the pigmies' cave," I exclaimed.

He sprahg from his chair, and stood staring at me with wide-open eyes.

"You must be mad," he cried.

"I thought so myself when I saw it," I replied. "Then you left me and I saw, between the picture and me, the living, substantial form of the girl I had found, loved, and lost."

He continued to stare at me with startled eyes.

"I strove to reach her, but fell—as you have since told me, down the stairs," I added.

"Halwood, is this life reality or a visionary dream?" he exclaimed. "Are we any of us responsible beings, or are we only playthings of Fate? Because," he continued, not waiting for me to reply, "either we are both mad, or we are experiencing something which knocks all the theories of personal responsibility into atoms."

"I don't know," I replied. "I only know that the image of the girl I found asleep in that cave fills my heart now, and is the one thing that will fill it till I find her. And that I do not expect to be able to do until I cross the barrier between this and the next world."

"But," he exclaimed excitedly, and then stopped, looking at me in a curious manner.

"There is something about this that you have not told me," I said quickly. "I have told you my story plainly and truthfully ; can you say the same?"

He sat down again and remained silent for

a time with his brow puckered in thought. Then he looked at me fairly in the eyes.

" No, I cannot," he said. " But I will now. I did not do so before, because it seemed to me to be so impossible. As things are turning out, I hardly know what to call it—absurd, miraculous, or visionary. Do you feel well enough to face that picture of my sister again ? I want to show you something, and we shall have to pass up the stairs."

" I believe I am strong enough," I answered.

" Then come," he answered, and together we left the room and proceeded along passages until we stood opposite the picture. I stopped and looked at it, but on a nearer inspection it struck me as being less like the image I had in my mind than when I first noticed it, and I said so to my companion.

" What is the difference ? " he inquired.

" The mouth seems different, and the eyes are too hard. The girl I seek has a mouth with lips that are full and soft, but yet with a good deal of strength in their curves, while her eyes are dreamy and dark—not blue, like those," and I nodded towards the picture.

He looked at me with the same curious expression on his face that I had noticed before.

" Let us go on," he said quietly, and he

resumed his walk, leading me into a room just off the passage.

It was a fairly large room, and was lit by two large windows at the end; but it was absolutely bare of furniture, with the exception of an artist's easel, on which there was a draped canvas.

"Tell me who this is," he said as he walked to the easel and threw back the drapery from the front of the canvas.

I started back with a cry. Painted on the canvas, with bold, daring skill, and looking at me with almost living eyes, I saw the portrait of my own face.

"Who painted that?" I exclaimed.

"Come back to our chairs and I will complete my story," he replied as he let the drapery fall again.

We went back to the room where we had been sitting, and as I listened to him I could do little else than echo his question, "Is life a reality, or are we only the playthings of Fate?"

CHAPTER XXVII.

THE LAST CALL.

"Before my sister's child was born," he began, "she had passed through that terrible ordeal of having her home shattered, her life wrecked, and her fair name betrayed by the man she had loved. More than that, in the overthrow of her own fortunes, she also saw those of her father and of his family overwhelmed. I do not want to speak harshly of the man you regard as a friend; but this I will say, that had I known who he was at the time that he offered me the chance of sharing in the wealth you two had discovered, my answer would have been a blow."

He spoke bitterly and with a hard ring in his voice, and I felt that what he was speaking was the truth. For some minutes he remained silent, and I did not care to interrupt his thoughts.

"Well, the child was born," he went on presently. "And then my sister's troubles in

329

this world were at an end. Then my father and brother followed her and I went to Australia; so that what I know of the child up to the time I came home again is, of course, hearsay only. My father's sister took charge of her— for it was a daughter—and with the influences that surrounded her mother before the little one came, it is not so very extraordinary that even as a babe the child should have been peculiar.

"She has not——" I began, when he held up his hand, and I stopped.

"She was—well, peculiar," he continued. "At the time when she should have been light-hearted and full of childish whims, she was quiet and listless. The ordinary childish amusements had no attractions for her, and her chief delight, if one can call it so, seems to have been the wandering about in the fields and lanes by herself. If any one were with her she used to remain stolid and pre-occupied; and when she did say anything it was only to give expression to ideas which would have been more appropriate for an old woman in her second childhood than for an innocent little five-year-old. Once, they tell me, she and her aunt were walking down a lane, when she found a dead sparrow lying on the footpath. The child stopped and picked it up, smoothing its feathers as it lay in her hand. Her aunt told her to throw it away, and she looked up and asked why. 'It is a nasty dead thing ; throw it away,' her aunt repeated. The poor little creature burst out crying. 'It is only asleep,' she said tearfully. 'Why is it nasty because it is asleep ?' 'It is dead,' her aunt told her. 'Dead ? What is dead ?' the child asked. Her aunt told her that she would understand when she was older ; but that would not satisfy the child, and in the end her aunt had to take the sparrow away and throw it over the hedge. For days the poor little thing fretted for her sparrow ; and, to console her, they bought her a big new doll. But she would not look at it. 'It is not even asleep. Take it away ; it is a deader thing than my sparrow,' she told them.

"When she grew older she grew even more peculiar. She did not care for any companions, and used to sit for hours staring away into space in a dreamy, listless way, until they thought she was going into melancholia. So they had doctors to see her ; but none of them could say anything more than that she wanted rousing, and to have some interest in life. At her school work she was clever, and at music and painting she showed more than ordinary talent—only she would not develop it. To a certain extent she followed instruction ; but just as she was beginning to make some real progress she would break away and follow her own ideas, which were usually such as to be incomprehensible to any one save herself. In playing she used to leave the music that was given her to learn severely alone ; and, instead of practising it, she used to strum such wild, doleful things, making them up as she went along, that they used to upset every one who heard them, and especially the old aunt, and the result was that the music tuition had to be abandoned. It was the same when they tried to teach her drawing. She scorned the copies set her after she had mastered the elementary part of the work ; and, instead, used to waste the paper with crude sketches of the most gruesome-looking objects. So they stopped that too.

" Her aunt was rather religious ; but poor Maggie used to horrify the old lady with her opinions upon Church and theological matters. When she was old enough to be confirmed the vicar tried his hand at her ; but he had to quit the task. She was too many for him ; though where she got the ideas she held puzzled every one. He gave her up in despair after a time, and told her aunt that she was worse than the veriest heathen ; and the only excuse for her was that her intellect was weak. And yet she was the gentlest creature possible, if any one were ill or in pain. It was not her fault that she was so peculiar ; it was her ideas, not her nature ; for she never grumbled or complained, even when they interfered with her strange amusements, and tried to rally her into something like any other ordinary, common-place girl. Perhaps if they had left her alone, she might have astonished them ; but the old aunt belongs to the old-fashioned school, and believes that every girl should be built on the same model. Poor Maggie, I believe, tried hard in her own way to do what was wanted of her, but her way was not understood ; and so she was alternately blamed and pitied, until she ceased even to try, and fell ill through it all. What took place before she was born is to blame for it all, I think," he added sadly.

" Is she still like that ? " I asked, touched by the dejection in his voice and on his face.

" She fell ill," he went on, ignoring my query. " The doctors urged a long sea trip, as a means of rousing her from the despondent state she had fallen into. They took her abroad, though it was a big strain on their income.   But it certainly did her good in one way, for when she came back she was not so sad and despondent.   Instead of her listless apathy, she seemed to be taking some interest in what was going on around her, and tried hard to carry out the little tasks which her aunt thought formed a proper occupation for her mind and hands.   The trip they took was on a mail liner as far as Ceylon and back, and it was on the homeward journey that she first showed signs of improvement.   The bright, clear, warm air of the tropics seemed to cheer her, and her aunt was congratulating herself that there was some hope for the poor thing after all.   There might have been, if they had only left her to herself, and allowed her to live out her life in her own strange way ; but they do not appear to have been able to understand that.   It is what I have done since I came over, and although there is not very much improvement so far, Maggie is no worse, and I believe that with another trip into a warm climate we shall be able to get her back, at all events to the point where she was when they interfered with her and her ideas, and upset her the last time."

"Poor girl," I said ; for the story of her unfortunate existence—another result of the

Hatter's unreasoning folly, I thought—affected me, and for the moment I was thinking of nothing else.

"It was such a simple thing too, as it appeared then," he went on. "She had somehow obtained possession of some colours and brushes, and over an old oleograph she had painted that picture I just showed you."

"My portrait!" I exclaimed.

"She had kept it perfectly secret from every one," he continued, not heeding my interruption. "But they found it out somehow, and then, watching her, discovered that she used to sit in front of it every night talking to it, and telling it how she had been trying all the day to do what they wanted her to do and fighting her besetting sins, as her aunt and the clergyman called them. Foolishly, they let her know that they had found it, and from that day she went back into her lonely, silent listlessness. When I came back and hunted them up and heard all about it, I made them bring it out, for they had hidden it away from her, and I nearly dropped when I saw who it was like. That is why I was so startled when you came here."

"Go on," I said, as he stopped. I felt myself growing more and more excited at his recital but compelled myself to listen.

"I have had medical experts to see her," he went on sadly; "but they do no good. All they say is that she wants rousing. Then I had that picture put in the room, where it is now. When she wants to go and look at it she can; only she does not even seem to care about that now. She seems to be either in a deep lethargy or in a state of utter indifference. She either sits all day in a state of almost trance, when she neither heeds nor hears, or else she regards everybody and everything with dreamy listlessness; and, if she speaks at all, it is always in a tone that suggests to me the idea that she is a body without a soul."

"Tell me," I exclaimed, as I heard his words and a thought flashed through my brain; " you say that she was different on her way home. Where was she then? Quick! Tell me."

"They first noticed it in the Suez Canal," he answered.

"In the—when, when? Tell me. She was ——it——I."

My tongue could not frame the thought in words, for over me and through me there was surging a flood of emotion so intense, so overwhelming, that I could only articulate in disjointed incoherency, as I sprang to my feet and stared wildly at my companion.

Coventry jumped up and laid his hand on me.

"Steady, old man, steady," he said quickly. "Keep cool or——I should not have told you. It will——"

But his words fell on ears that scarcely heard them, for as he spoke the door on the opposite side of the room opened and there, framed in the portal, stood the form I had seen standing between me and the picture in the passage above the stairs.

She was looking straight at me, with a soft sweet smile playing round her lips and, as she stood, I saw two others come up behind her, an elderly lady and the nurse who had attended to me. I saw them take hold of her arms and try to lead her away ; but she stood firm, looking at me.

"William," I heard the elderly woman exclaim, and Coventry turned. "My God ! what have you done ? " he cried, as he sprang towards them.

The appealing softness in her lovely eyes thrilled through me with delight, and I stood drinking it in, lost in the ecstasy of the moment, till I saw that they were dragging her back. Then I found my senses, and with a wild cry also sprang forward, shouting the words that had come to me twice before :

" Naggah ! Naggah !　Oom-moo-hah ! "

The girl scarcely seemed to move, but she flung the three of them from her, and was crouching at my feet, sobbing and crying in a fit of hysterical abandon, before they realised what she was doing.

With my uninjured arm I raised her, and she clung to me with her arms round my neck, and her head pillowed on my shoulder.　I looked at the three who were in the doorway, and over them and around them it seemed to me that some dark influence hung.

" The folly of man is measured," I cried, feeling my heart throbbing with a sense of victorious elation.　" The power of destiny has won."

I felt the girl's head lift from my shoulder, and, glancing down, my eyes met hers.　I bent my head till our lips touched.

What it was I know not, but even as I stood in that old English house, holding the girl in my embrace, I was conscious in all the vividness of actual reality, of being once more upon that distant, desert ridge, kneeling by the side of the slumbering form of her whom I had found in that strangely illumined cavern ; but only the form was visionary and unreal, while the living entity was in a luminous presence beside me, and with me. A sense of ineffable gladness came upon me as the vision passed, and left me conscious of only one state of being, that of standing in the room of old Saxted Manor, a physical man with a material environment, and with a living, breathing woman clinging to me.

"At last, at last," she was saying. "The darkness and solitude have passed, for you, my love, have come to me."

*   *   *   *   *

The medical experts said it was a complete vindication of their theory that my lovely Margaret only needed rousing from her lethargic apathy to become the bright, happy, intelligent woman she now is. But she and I, in the sweet communion of our perfect love, look together in awe-struck solemnity at the fleeting vista of dimly realised scenes and memories which seem to blend the living present with a bygone past. And we strive to understand something of the subtle chain which links the mystery of the present with the far-off eternal mists of changeless Time.

THE END.

Printed by Hazell, Watson, & Viney, Ld., London and Aylesbury.

Printed in the United States
21007LVS00002B/43-194